The Land of No Return

The Land of No Return

Bhima Prusty

Translated by
Dr. Tapan K Panda

BLACK EAGLE BOOKS
Dublin, USA | Bhubaneswar, India

Black Eagle Books
USA address:
7464 Wisdom Lane
Dublin, OH 43016

India address:
E/312, Trident Galaxy, Kalinga Nagar,
Bhubaneswar-751003, Odisha, India

E-mail: info@blackeaglebooks.org
Website: www.blackeaglebooks.org

First International Edition Published by
Black Eagle Books, 2023

THE LAND OF NO RETURN
by **Bhima Prusty**
Translated by **Dr. Tapan K Panda**

Original Copyright © Bhima Prusty
Translation Copyright © Dr. Tapan K Panda

Cover: **Madhur Singh Pradhan**
Interior Design: Ezy's Publication

ISBN- 978-1-64560-482-2 (Paperback)
Library of Congress Control Number: 2023950941

Printed in the United States of America

Jambu- The Land of No Return

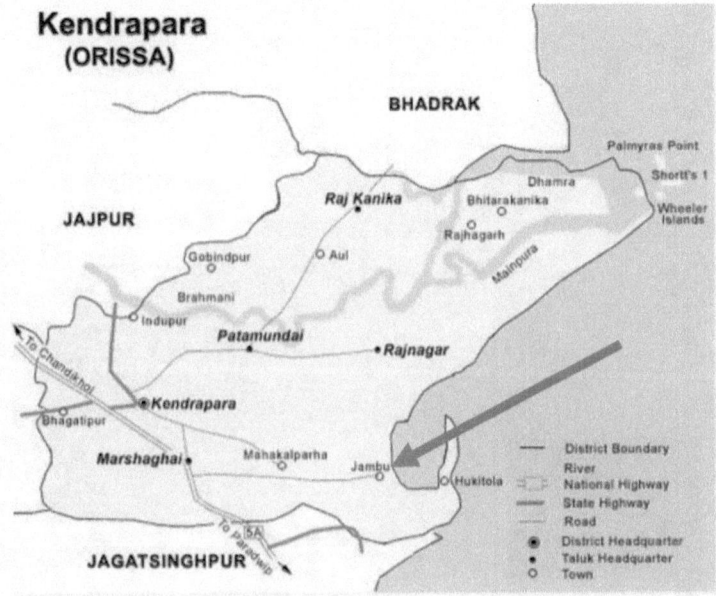

The Land of No Return

Writing a spot novel based on-field experiences alongside the visuals - vision has a greater significance than collating information from readings and listening to everyday musings. Before writing *Jambu*loka, my other novels like *Muhaan, Om, Kabita ra Upannyas*, and *Odisha Sahitya Academy-winning Samudra Manisha*' are the harvest of years of on-ground research. *Jambu*loka is also a novel based on a field investigation of displacement and migration. The characters of this novel are real and hold the actual names of people from *Jambu*. The storyline is based on their language, emotions, practices, and rituals.

'Place' is essential for me to write a novel based on my on-field experiences. Suppose you make the 'place' as your protagonist. It is natural for the people living there to become characters in the novel. You can fetch the story of a book from their everyday life. I have experimented with the same in this novel.

'Before writing this novel, during an informal chat with friends in one of the evenings, the subject of the existence of *Jambu* in *Kendrapada* district came into the discussion. This place is like a Mini-*Bangladesh*. This connotation of *Bangladesh* being in *Odisha* stuck with me for a long time. Finally, I started mentally preparing to make a trip to *Jambu* to visit this place and interact with the people. *Ravi Tripathy*- a friend from *Chandbali*, had already visited *Jambu* several times. He was around to help me to get there. We started on a motorbike. After crossing the *Baitarani River* and passing through places like *Raj Kanika, Ali, and Pattamundai*, it was almost late evening when we arrived at *Jambu*.

On the banks of the river *Gobari*, completely engulfed in the darkness and amongst tall trees- lay our dream island- *Jambu*! We only knew someone before this visit who could help us with a night stay. Loading our bike on a country boat, we reached the other side of *Jambu*-popularly called *Jambunut*. *Ravi Tripathy* had an earlier acquaintance with *Govind Senapati*- the *khalas*i (loader) of the irrigation department who lived in a tile-roofed government quarter. There was hardly any facility for water and power. Spreading our mats on the floor, we spent the night brimming about visiting *Jambu*. The next day, riding a boat on the *Gobari* River, we were in *Jambu* to meet many unknown people who later became part of the *Jambu* Saga.

Finding time from my academic life between 2010 and 2017, I continued solo travelling to *Jambu* multiple times. There, I was introduced to *Sri Samarendra Mohanty*-a *television* reporter from the *Chhapali Chowk*. He could comprehend my working style and extended full cooperation to me. In those seven years, as many times I visited *Jambu*, my reporter friend *Sri Mohanty* arranged my stay at varied places- government bungalows, forest bit houses, even in his own home. He had taken me to many places around *Jambu* like a kind-hearted guide.

Along with *Jambu*, he had arranged my visit to *Ramnagar*

Kharnasi, Odisha's first lighthouse, and to *Hukitola-* the first port of *Odisha.* Through a generous introduction to forest guards and rangers of the area, he helped me to understand the topography and lifestyle of the *Jambu* people. I could have many exciting conversations with younger and older people from different *Bangladeshi* hamlets and colonies through his kind introductions of me to the *Jambu* people.

I tried to tape-record the life and struggle of the people of *Jambu. Binoy Das,* who was displaced during the civil war and riots in erstwhile *East Bengal* and finally could settle in *Jambu,* often turns nostalgic and talks about his struggling days; the cloth merchant turned Indian nationalist *Bakul Talukdar;* the youth leader *Nimain Sarjan* who raises his concern and voice for the issues and rights of the refugee brotherhood living in *Jambu; Tapan Sikdar* who, after being tortured in *Bangladesh,* along with his family had to leave the country and have greyed in *Jambu; Madhoi Mandol* who was damn scared after receiving an expulsion notice from the Indian government for illegal entry into India; *Kadamb Sena,* with nine months pregnancy fled the country during the *East Bengal* and *Pakistan* civil war and arrived here. I tried to record the lifestyle and life stories of hundreds of people of *Jambu,* like *Jatia* of Kharnasi village and octogenarian *Purjan Mandal.*

Only one common malice of these refugees in *Jambu* inspired me to write this novel. *Jambu* has seen three generations since the 1960s. They have an unresolved question: Which nation do they belong to? The country they left a long time ago or the country in which they have been living for generations!! One nation brands expatriates, and another government names them as 'refugees'. Wherever there is a civil war, a religious war, or a political war related to international borders, people are bound to cross the geographic boundaries as refugees for their own and kin's safety and welfare. The issues of displacement and refugees are global phenomena. *Jambu* may be a tiny place on the world map of immigration and refugee settlement. Still, *Jambu* continues to be a mini-representative of refugee colonies of the world. After arriving at these colonies, including *Jambu*, There is no way open to going back. *Jambu* is the Land of No Return!!!

While acquainting myself with *Jambu* and its people for writing this novel and describing its history, ethos, and culture, keeping people's life stories in the backdrop, I had to read books on the history of *Bangladesh*, check statistics on the arrival of *Bengali* refugees in India; gather information on whereabouts of the lighthouse; planning documents of *Hukitola* Port and autobiography of John Beams. It was possible to write a realistic novel from ground zero by discussing and recording conversations and rich experiences of the people of *Jambu*, their history, and their current status.

After completing the novel *Jambuloka*, the manuscript was recognized by the *Tapasya Foundation* with "*Tapasya Srujan Puraskar*". The foundation published the novel in 2017. Later on. *Dr Tapan K Panda* translated the book' *Jambuloka*" as "*The Land of No Return*" into English for a global audience. I am grateful to the people who seeded the idea of *Jambu*, helped me reach *Jambu*, and introduced me to the commoner of *Jambu* and *Dr. Panda* for translating this novel.

It is like a dream and a matter of immense happiness for an author that his book will reach a larger audience to read about a place and its people. Let the world read *The Land of No Return*. Let the world come and see *Jambu*.

Bhima Prusty

To Which Country Do I Belong?

The Land of No Return (*Jambuloka* in Odia) has a special place in my heart. This is for varied reasons, and I will only do justice to the novel if I write about the same. Five years before, I wished to make a film on climate change, read many books, and watch movies based on issues related to climate change. I have published extensively on sustainability and circular economy and wanted to use the visual medium for a more impactful conversation on the imminent danger of global warming and climate change. That is when Dr Arun Pradhan (Husband of my dear friend Dr Hiranmayaee Mishra) gave me a photocopy of the novel 'Samudra Manisha' by Sri Bhima Prusty. Reading that novel was so great that I presented Sri Prusty's field research at many international conferences, including the workshop I did for Meta (Facebook) as part of my fellowship. It was a completely different experience to see the author's style, structure and format through his series of spot novels. It was less of a fiction and more of a field investigation for me.

Then, the Tapasya Foundation decided to set up awards in the field of literature. In the first year, this manuscript, 'Jambuloka', won the Tapasya Srujan Puraskar. That's when I met the original author. I was blown away by his simplicity, commitment and effort in shaping his novels. I thank Dr. Hiranmayee for this manuscript. I remember my first meeting with jury members- when they asked me how different your selection process is from other awards, my answer was simple- unique, focused, and a trendsetter. That's what this novel is all about.

This novel 'Jambuloka' was published by Tapasya Foundation as a part of the award and through Paschima Publications. The same story bagged 'The Sarala Award' by IMFA this year. This announcement strengthened our belief that we have not gone wrong in selecting this novel for the Tapasya Award.

I have been translating Odia novels into English for a broader, global audience. I took my own swift time to complete this translation as I carefully chose the words and scenes described in the original. It is almost impossible to match the repertoire of Sri Bhima Prusty in the original novel. However, I have seen several videos of Jambu and other refugee settlements to experience the issues and challenges the people face. I wonder if the world could have been without national boundaries. However, I decided to visit Jambu and go through all the places mentioned by the author before I chose to translate. I made it after COVID-19 and could visualize the spots mentioned by the author. The visit helped me a lot while working on the novel.

The Land of No Return (Original as *Jambuloka*) is a novel that depicts the plight, insecurity, and anxiety of *Bangladesh*i refugees who left *East Bengal* in fear of saving their lives, respect, and honour. The novel has eight chapters that describe the incidents, disquiet, struggle, and optimism. Still, in between, there is an entire flow of pathos and agony.

The story's background is politics, history, religion,

economics, the catastrophe of a civil war, and the role of an ugly anarchy. There is also a reference to Indira Gandhi, who supported *Bangladesh*'s Freedom (*Mukti*) Movement, which created a base for a new political balance theorization in South Asia; with the arrival of the people from *Bangladesh* in India, a new culture and life began for them. The people who left *East Bengal* and settled at *Jambu* have developed from a sapling into a tree. Still, they carry their memories with them, which have given them hope to live.

Modern writers like Sri *Bhima Prusty*, right from the beginning of being realistic, have theorized politics as an essential aspect of contemporary life and writing as a medium of communication of the common man's despair. The novel *Jambuloka* is a signature of *Sri Bhima Prusty*, who spends months and years collecting data, researching on the ground, and blending creativity into a real and meaningful storyline.

I thank Sri Bhima Prusty for allowing me to translate this novel into English and agreeing to the title 'The Land of No Return'. Young artist and my friend and story writer Chirashree Indrasingh's daughter, Madhur Singh Pradhan, decided to do the cover. This is a classic painting aptly done by her to match the novel. My sincere thanks to Madhur. Sri Satya Patnaik and Black Eagle Books have a shared vision- working towards globalizing Odia literature for a broader audience. He has agreed to publish the novel, and I am grateful. A novel's beauty and readability go higher with how the book is designed. Sri Ashok Parida has painstakingly taken on this task, and I thank him.

While working on this novel, I had many questions on war, politics and society in general, which I bounced upon with my wife and political sociologist Dr Julie Mishra during our conversations. She has kept these conversations live and warm with her thoughts on the refugee crisis. So, thanks to her for sensitizing me to this global issue.

Despite all efforts to do the translation, I understand that some inaccuracy and error may have cropped up due to the monumental work of entirely shifting such a classic novel into a foreign language- so I owe all the mistakes and lapses. I hope you will like the translation and will always remember the question asked by one of the characters in the novel: The country which we fled from calls us expatriates; the government where we took shelter calls us refugees. To which country do we belong?

Happy Reading!!

Dr. Tapan K. Panda
15th November, 2023

VIEWS on JAMBULOKA

While reading 'Indira's Signature', I recalled the incidents that happened twenty-five to thirty years back. There was a deposit of saline water in *Bani* and the marshy land as the water couldn't recede into the sea. In between was a small parcel of land that appeared like an island. There were narrow paths to walk. I had met the refugee family there who hailed from *East Bengal.* The family includes a middle-aged couple. The husband does fishing. His wife also catches fish and crabs, cleans prawns, and cook's food at home. For a few days, in a nearby place, I stayed among these people who do fish business, and it was not for the *Bhekti* fish or the *Bagda* prawn but to watch these families closely!

They were mostly silent and didn't have the botheration of having children. I have never seen them speaking to each other. They always appeared sad! I tried to find out the reason. It might have happened that they left their near and dear ones in *Khulna's Bagharhat* village. They might have met in a refugee camp. They might have thought of starting the family life together to get support, overcome their loneliness, or come out of their sadness. Now, while reading this novel, they might be recalling their past. They might discuss their village, the trees, siblings, and family. For them, no one exists now. They have begun a new chapter in their life in a new place. These are the reasons for them to be silent and remorseful.

It is like a hide-and-seek game. The ultimate truth is about survival in this world. This may not be in *Bagarhat's* ancestral house -the old building constructed by the Britishers. Let it be in *Jambu's* marshy land. That's the reason why *Rai Babu* supported Indira. There was safety and security. The whole system itself is like a sore that will never heal. Flying to *Jambu* with the beheaded President *Yahiya Khan* is hilarious. A desire bloomed during the freedom and language movement in the depth of the mind, and a passion blossomed within. It's not a small thing at all. Initially, writing a small chapter of ten pages narrating the travel from *Khulna* to *Jambu* and settling them there is challenging. Those ten pages also include a bloody war, the monarchy, the internal politics of India, the foreign policy, from *Sam Manekshaw* to Kissinger, America's Nixon government's behaviour and Russia's support, and *Mukti Bahini's* victory.

As an author, you have tried your best to write concisely about one of the turning points in history so fast and with so much clarity that it appears like a video film! You always write in this way. Congratulations on your keen observation. It is said that you can't write a novel unless you imagine. Still, you have differentiated the thin line between real and imaginary. It is easier for the reader to find out if there is something fictional at the novel's end. You are a craftsman who has weaved his thoughts like a goldsmith for the minute filigree work. Right from *Mahima Matha* to *Hukitola*, you have vividly described the incidents in a superb flow. The depiction of human life is incredible. You must know that *Surendra Mohanty's 'Neti Neti'* novel's first few chapters were also written in the same style, which finally took the shape of a novel so that small stories can be conceived by considering the first few chapters.

While reading the novel, I remembered *Taslima Nasrin* and her novel *'Phera'*, an amazingly touching story woven around the life of a young girl and the struggle between her past and present in a very heart-touching way. Other than *Rai Babu*, the other characters are symbols of dependence. What can be said about them? Let from the ashes rise the phoenix. I pray for the long life of the child born into *Bholanath's* family.

Late Sri Bibhuti Bhusan Pradhan

Author- Dheu, Nata, and Badhi

This creation of *Bhima Prusty* (in the form of a novel) significantly contributes to Odia literature for three reasons. One is the political aspect, and the second is the entry of the immigrants into the state of *Odisha*- to the new villages and the society; finally, the third reason is its core structure, which talks about forming a society- a displaced society.

There is hardly any novel based on political issues in *Odia*. Stereotypical novels revolving around political problems don't draw the attention of *Odia* readers as they are not romantic.

Modern writers like *Bhima*, right from the beginning of being realistic, have theorized politics as an essential aspect of life. In that process, with Indira Gandhi's leadership supporting *Bangladesh*'s Freedom Movement, a base was created for a new theory of political balance. This attempt by *Bhima Prusty* is commendable. With the arrival of the people from *Bangladesh*, a new culture and way of life were introduced. It's a unique depiction of the *Odia* novel world. *Bhima Prusty*, through his creation, has entangled my mind with many questions. What is not mentioned in the story, I imagined it and wondered. The political metaphor in his novel may mean that. Indira Gandhi gave the *Bengali* home a lot of importance in this creation. What is exactly that? Is it the pain of losing the motherland or only a political issue? It is difficult to infer. The silent radio and the wound that will never heal are the two metaphors that aren't entirely developed. In another way, *Bhima Prusty* has not allowed these metaphors to stand alone. It could be the way the plot is conceived.

To convert the forest land into farmland that can be used for farming and growing crops reflects the past civilization. It's not enough to convey this meaning through an imaginary creation; instead, it is necessary to elaborate through a novel based on it. What is the reason why the sore and the continuous radio playing couldn't be the centre of this creation?

Hara Prasad Das
Poet and Author of Vamsa, Garva Griha and Harlem Ra Rati

This novel is based on a small story titled 'Indira's Signature'. I began reading it that way, but after reading it, I realized it's a part of a grand novel called *Jambuloka'*. The essence of the story will be lost if we see it on the larger canvas of the novel.

This novel is more relevant and rational and explains human suffering and pain. The way the novel is conceived is highly appreciable. It's a beautiful creation in Odia literature, and I am sure it will have its own independent existence. Its thrust area is not limited to romance or relationships. It goes beyond place and time, and the depth of the treatment is commendable.

A person cannot be confined to a place forcibly, nor can the thoughts be restricted to physical boundaries. This is what listlessness means. The characteristics of completeness in the novel's storyline, identity, and protagonist perception are well structured. The novel is beautifully conceived and engaging and can potentially create anxiety among readers on what to do next. The storyline also involves national and international issues. The story's background is geopolitics, history, religion, regional economics, catastrophic war effects, and an ugly monarchy's role.

The victims of such a complex historical event made

many people lose their independence and culture. They revolted against the ruler, lost their motherland, and took shelter in another country as refugees. The storyline has evolved from the anxiety of the common man.

The author is a writer who has the uncanny ability to perceive the pain and agony of the people and bring them into his storyline. The novelist has tried his best, and the same confidence has placed you as a unique and different writer. A novel based on facts and reality is difficult to find as the writer has taken an off-beat road. The author has used the locally spoken colloquial language. I know this is your style – to talk in the language of the people you write about.

Padmaj Pal
Author of Kuade Jibaara Nahin, Devdasi and Paapa Pari Nijara

The original story 'Indira's Signature' on which this novel is based can't only be said to have 'migration' and 'human resettlement' as the unique theme. The signature speaks about the most critical element of a complex social issue, without which the signature is meaningless.

This signature symbolizes displacement, which began in *Khulna* in *East Bengal* and ended in *Jambu* in *Odisha*. Displacement and refugee movement is a complex global problem that has spread its wings with branches entangled with the future of human civilization. As a reader, we are affected by any of the character's happiness and sorrow; the incidents are narrated as pathetic stories, like a canvas painted with the despair of the human race.

The story describes *Rai Babu's* beliefs, his radio, and the cleaning of the marshy forest land to develop a settlement. It ends with the celebration of the birth of *Bholanath's* grandson. Among all this misery, they have always tried to overcome life's difficulties and have never been defeated in their attempt to survive. The sore in *Rai Babu's* feet will never heal, and so will his pain. A story based on displacement is always very complicated as it depicts the agony and pain of people and slowly becomes a part of history. In our civilization, a human being is like a sapling who can sustain himself/herself regardless of which condition you pitch them against. This is a story of struggle and optimism; in between, there is a path to pathos. As the story progresses, the people who left *Khulna* and settled in *Jambu* have grown from a sapling into a tree. This tree carries its memories with them, giving them hope to live in the future.

In this novel by *Bhima Prusty*, Indira Gandhi is livelier than in reality. This novel depicts in the same way a poet gives life to the entity in a poem. Indira Gandhi has given them places and hopes to live, and that's why they have a close attachment to Indira. They have lived a life of struggle in their own country before displacement and have lived in this country after the migration with similar pain. Though the original story is named 'Indira's Signature', the signature of the writer *Bhima Prusty* has blown the original into this beautiful novel. The story is based on the marginalization of refugees in a society where a group of people must live with a sore that will never heal. This is the genuine signature. Anyone who knows how to sign can always put his signature, and *Bhima Prusty* has shined through his signature style in this novel.

Jyoti *Nanda*
Author of Ekadaa Eka Dina

I spent much of my life across the nation and the globe. After reading the novel, I felt like I was one of the refugees in this world. This work is dedicated to millions of refugees who lost everything – just to survive.

Dr. Tapan K. Panda

Chapter-1

At a time when Europe is inundated by refugees escaping violence and wars in Syria, Libya, and other Middle Eastern countries, the world could, perhaps, learn a lesson or two from India's experience of holding a 10 million refugee crisis on its land 46 years ago.

-Indira's Signature

It was midnight in *Khulna's Bagerhat* village.

A few Muslim people came and assembled in our courtyard. The *Maulavi* of the village knocked at the door and called, *'Rai Babu! Rai Babu!'*.

My Grandfather was petrified. He got up from the bed, tying his *Doria **lungi***. We never thought that there would be a ransack. The ladies of our house will be humiliated. The ladies were scared, and they kept the children along with them and locked themselves in the house. What will happen at night? We were all scared.

The Muslim leader of the village, *Khabir Mian*, stood outside the house and said- 'I am *Khabir*. Please open the door, *Rai Babu*. I have to speak to you something important.'

My Grandfather was a freedom fighter, so the Hindus and Muslims in the village and nearby areas respected him. We were known to all as we belonged to *Rai Babu's* family. Many Muslims respected my Grandfather and wished him *Salam, Khuda Hafiz*. My father and uncles had betel and betel nut businesses spread over half of the *Khulna* district. With that strength, my Grandfather stopped my father and uncles and said- 'Wait! Let me check,' and he opened the door. He saw many known Muslim people standing there without weapons, but there was a reflection of guilt on their faces.

Khabir Mian said-'*Rai Babu*! It's not safe for your family to stay here. We have come to know that the miscreants from the city have reached the village and are planning to attack your house. In that case, neither the *Maulavi* nor the villagers can help and save your family from them. If we try to protect your family, our people will be killed. We have come here at this time to caution you. Kindly keep in mind that others shouldn't come to know about it. There is a boat which is already ready near the river *Bairabh*. Kindly leave this place at the earliest. It will be suitable for all by the grace of Allah!'

They vanished in the darkness. It was like a thunderstorm that fell on my Grandfather, father, and uncles. -*Where will we go, leaving the property, business, and the money given on loan?* There was no answer to this question. All of us assembled near our Grandfather. He took the decision and said helplessly that he had to leave *Bagerhat* village and *East Bengal*. We have to leave our property, house, and relatives behind. We were destined to stay in our country only for this period. Whatever we can take along with us, arrange those.'

Where will we go?' My father asked my Grandfather, keeping his business in mind.

He said- 'Why are you asking that? We will go to *Indira's* country. We will get a refuge there and can save our lives. People have been taking refuge there since the 1958 riot. Now it's 1971- Lakhs of people from this country have taken refuge there and are doing business and leading a prosperous life. Won't we get a place in *Indira's* country?'

My father was annoyed with my Grandfather. He said 'the condition of *Indira* wasn't good in India. If we go there, we must stay in a refugee camp, and the life there is terrible.'

-'Do you want all of us to die here? If we stay here, then we have to face tyranny. They will torture our children and women folk. Do you want to stay here to go through all this? If you think that property and money matter, then tie a lungi instead of a *Dhoti*, grow a beard, stop praying to God and read *Namaz*, make the ladies wear a *Burkha*, start eating beef, and instead of the surname *Rai*, use *Khan*. This is the only way to stay here.'

These types of incidents were happening in *East Bengal*. Grandfather narrated it again to caution us. We all became quiet, listening to him, but my father still couldn't decide. He was hesitating about leaving *East Bengal* and living in another country. My Grandfather came near him and said –'Those inhuman people have an eye on our family. Where will we hide here in *East Bengal*? Is it possible to hide in relatives' houses and other districts? Do you think that the tyranny of Pakistan's military government over *East Bengal* will stop so soon? No, it will increase over time. If we stay here, all of us in the family will die. It's better to go to the refugee camp. Will *Indira* throw us away from there?

She has given refuge to many people from this country. We can live there without any fear.'

Grandfather sang a well-known *Baul song*, "It's our fate... We are empty-handed.' The pain and suffering of all men who had lost everything were hidden in that song. The smoke-chocked throat had a coarse rhythm and spiralled his despair. Grandfather said – 'Alas! My country, our golden Bengal.'

Towards the song's end, my Grandfather started whizzing as he couldn't release his pain through his weeping. Who will guide *Rai*'s family if the old man dies in this situation? We impatiently agreed to the proposal to go to *Indira*'s country.

Grandfather suddenly stopped whizzing. He sat straight, looked at us, and showed us a dream: 'Let's go and see *Indira*'s country. There is a hell and heaven difference between our country and her country.'

All of us felt like laughing. Grandfather is talking about India and *Indira* leaving behind the tales of *Dhaka* and *East Bengal*. He has gathered much information by reading the newspaper and listening to his old German-made radio. He read the famous newspapers of *East Bengal*, like *Prathama Alo, Kalerae Kanth, Amar Desh,* and *Samkal*. He gathered detailed information about *Indira* after *Jawaharlal Nehru*. He had even cut various photographs of *Indira* from the newspaper and had kept them carefully in his books. We knew he was very much attached to India and an ardent follower of *Indira*. Whenever there is a discussion about *Indira,* he listens to it carefully. He says-'*Indira* has married a Muslim, and all the Muslim houses are her in-law's house. *Indira* is not only a Muslim but also a Hindu. Won't a Hindu give refuge to a *Bengali* Hindu?'

The scary and weepy night was over, and I was listening to Indira's praise. As soon as it was the morning, we started packing our belongings to escape the tyranny of the *Bihari* Muslim ruffians.

After the evening, darkness spread its wings across the bank of the river *Bhairab*. It was so dark that we were all apprehensive- after how many days of travel would we end up where? Nobody had any idea! The boat and the boatmen were all ready. *Khabir Mian's* men had made all the necessary arrangements beforehand.

There were twelve to fourteen people who belonged to *Rai's* family. As we vacated the house, we saw many Muslim people walking along with us, and they were sad as we were leaving the country. A few were beating their chest, saying 'Hai Allah!". The Muslim ladies and the ladies of our house were crying. My mother and aunt were crying. The small kids thought that we were going to some relatives' house. We had de-roped ten to fifteen cattle behind in the yard. The cattle mooing made us mad, and the pain was unbearable. The benevolence and amity of a group of Muslims and the animosity of the other group remained a reminiscence forever in our hearts. We climbed the boat and left our motherland, leaving the last few drops of tears for the last time on the land.

While organizing the boat from the *Bairav* River towards the sea, the boatmen prayed to the famous *Khulna* goddess, *Khulnaswari*. We were discussing *Sheikh Mujibur Rahman's* struggle for freedom. After our boat passes through the Sundarbans, we will never be able to see the floating forest again. We waited eagerly, apprehending where the boat would leave us. My Grandfather was simultaneously listening to the

All India Radio and *Dhaka*'s Radio Station, swinging in the same boat tune. Wherever our boat landed, we were apprehensive about how our neighbours would treat us in the new place. We were floating in the diacritical songs of trust and doubt!

Grandfather made us listen to Indira's speech in the *Bangladeshi* refugee camp at high volume. We could hear *Indira* saying, "You have left your country and come to us to save yourself from injustice and tyranny. People can eliminate injustice and tyranny if they stay in their own country and fight against it. Our Hindustan is a poor country, but for those who have left their country and have come here, we extend a helping hand to them. We will do whatever is possible.'

After listening to *Indira's* speech, both father and son duo were silent. Grandfather asked his son in the boat: 'Do you trust me now after listening to Indira's speech in the refugee camp?' She is *Indira*. Her land is safer for us.'

We reached a place which was a dense forest. It was already morning in the boat itself. On one side was the vast river *Gobari* and the entangled marshy land on the other. Is this the country? Three government officials had come to take us from the boat to the camp. They took us to an old, two-story building constructed during British rule. There were already six to seven *Bangladeshi* families staying there before us. Is this the camp? The second floor of the building needed to be in habitable condition. The roof had cracked, and Banyan and *Peepul* trees had grown on the walls. The doors and windows were broken. There were few rooms downstairs that could only be used for sleeping at night.

The government officials gave the ration according to the family members and said – you can cook and have food.

Try to adjust to this camp; later on, you can enjoy all the facilities you have enjoyed in your country. Have patience for the time being.'

Grandfather signalled, 'Did you notice how the government officials of *East Bengal* are involved in the bloodshed? Here, the government officials are distributing relief to the refugees.' Like the other families in the refugee camp, my father and uncle made a hearth with bricks and mud. They brought the firewood from the forest. The house ladies started cooking, and the children were busy playing the popular *Gaadan* game of their country. The apprehensions that we had about the camp vanished like body sweat. The nine families, consisting of forty to fifty people who left their country petrified, slowly adjusted to *Jambu's* environment.

The old and young men of the camp decided that they would analyze the situation and behaviour of the government towards them and then decide whether to stay in the country; most of them assembled near *Rai Babu* to listen to the news on the radio.

Indira was giving her speech in the lower house of the parliament. A lady was raising her protest in the voice of a hundred male members -India doesn't want to interfere in the internal issues of Pakistan. We have never done this for the past twenty-three years, but Pakistan hasn't restrained from it. Today, what is said to be an internal issue in Pakistan has become an internal issue in India. The government of Pakistan has begun with 'Operation Searchlight,' a planned military action to curb nationalist movement in erstwhile *East Pakistan,* and almost three lakh people have lost their lives. To escape from the genocide, lakhs of people have come to our country and have taken refuge in *West Bengal, Tripura, Odisha, and Bihar*. It is difficult for us to take care of the refugees and save them from communal riots. The government is losing its grip on the refugee issue. That's why we firmly say to Pakistan that the steps it takes in the name of internal matters should be stopped immediately. The activities are not conducive for lakhs of people staying there and here in our country. Pakistan can't be given the liberty to do this.'

The people in the camp appreciated *Indira's* retort against the military rulers of Pakistan. Still, they eagerly awaited hearing about *Sheikh Mujibur Rahman* from *Dhaka's* Radio Station. They wanted to know about their fellow *Bengalis* in the country. The atrocities against the *Bengalis* had increased in leaps and bounds; he didn't want people to hear that, so he didn't turn on the *Dhaka* radio station. He listened to the news late at night about the cruelty and oppression of *Yahiya Khan* and cried in solitude. He tried to boost the morale of the people in the camp and made them listen to what *Indira* said. Whenever there was a discussion about *Indira*, he said- 'Listen! A few days back, *Indira* announced she would release *Bango Bandhu, Sheikh Mujibur Rahman*, from imprisonment. She said, 'We will extend our help to the liberation army *(Mukti Bahini)*, which is fighting the War of Liberation.'

The people in the camp were relaxed after listening to Indira's assurance. They said- Will *Indira* release our *Bango Bandhu?* Will peace and harmony return to *our **Sonar Bangla*** (Golden Bengal)? Can we ever go back to our country leaving this camp?

My Grandfather told the people- 'there would be peace in *East Bengal*, not for the leaders there but for *Indira*.'

-'How'? People argued-'Where will our *Bengali* friends

go? Where will our *Mukti Bahini* go? What will result from the sacrifice of lakhs of *Bengali* people?'

My Grandfather smiled and said, 'Idiots! Can't you understand? Who is inspiring the *Mukti Bahini*, which is engaged in guerrilla warfare?'

People asked- 'Who'?

Grandfather said- '*Indira*'. It's only *Indira* who is doing this. Though she is in her own country, she is instrumental in forming the *Mukti Bahini* in our country and supporting the guerrilla warfare to liberate our country. *Sam Manekshaw* - the Army General of India, has sent the soldiers in disguise to our country and set up secret training camps to train the people. *Bengali* people, *Bangladesh Rifle Bahini*, social workers, and intelligentsia want *Bangladesh* to be separated from Pakistan through the *Mukti Bahini*. Every month, twenty thousand guerrillas are trained in the camp. *Indira*, along with *Manekshaw*, is providing arms and ammunition to them and has named them *Mukti Bahini*. With the arms and ammunition supplied by India, the people of our country are fighting to make the country independent. *Indira* controls everything from India like pushing a switch, and the guerrilla war is being fought in *Bangladesh*.'

People couldn't understand the deeper meaning of what their Grandfather talked about after listening to stuff on the radio. They desperately wanted the war to end as soon as possible so that they could return to their country. There was only one reply from Grandfather- 'This shadow war isn't going to end so soon. Pakistan will never let our *East Bengal* go from its hand so quickly. There will be more bloodshed. The military rule will destroy the country, and everything will turn into ashes. It will be over only after the whole country is destroyed. It may take some time for the government to again rise from the ashes like a Phoenix.'

Our country was on fire, and on the other hand, we were staying in the old abandoned bungalow in that marshy land and counting our days. Some government officials came to the camp one day with few official files. They measured the number of people staying in the centre per family. They left, saying- 'the marshy forest land of *Jambu* will be cleared, and a hut will be provided to each family. All of you will stay in your own houses and leave the camp. Fifty rupees per month will be given to each family for their maintenance. This is an order from the Indian government.'

People in the camp were perturbed as they would get only fifty rupees per family from the government. In a few families, there were more than fifteen people. How will they manage with fifty rupees? How will they purchase rice, groceries, vegetables, and medicines for the family in that forest? There were no shops in the nearby areas. For purchases, they must go to *Kujanga, Marsaghai, or Kendrapada*. There was no transport facility. They must cross the river *Gobari* and walk for ten to fifteen miles.

We were fearful as we left all the facilities and came here, inviting trouble in life's deep, cold mud. My Grandfather went to the gathering, hanging his transistor, holding his walking stick in hand, and said gleefully, "Did you see? What did I say? *Indira* has given shelter to us; now she will provide us with houses.'

-'What about getting only fifty rupees monthly?' The camp's most talkative and blabber mouth, *Kunipada Biswas*, asked. Grandfather was visibly annoyed and said- 'it was not a big thing that *Indira* gave us refuge in her country and is sheltering us. I think the reason why she is giving us less money is an issue for you people. Do you know there are one crore *Bangladeshi* refugees in India at present? There are almost three hundred crores of liability in this country. This is a big country with a large population. Will they sustain or not? Do you think *Indira* will spend everything on the refugees and weaken India economically?'

Rai Babu's talks are like this only. He made others shut up whoever spoke like this about *Indira*. Though he could convince others, the old man was worried for his family. The reason for his worry was his middle-aged son whose daughters weren't married. There were no suitable matches for them. There were no schools here for the school-going children. Children were roaming in the camp and around the bank of the river without studies like wanderers. The environment around the camp didn't suit the ladies in the house. Their maternal homes were in *East Bengal*. The ladies are more dominant in a *Bengali* family's bedroom. My father and uncle were in the chorus of returning to home town. My Grandfather tried to convince them in his way, saying- 'I have left that land and will never return. I will stay here.'

The old man went to jail during the *Bhasa Andolan* (language revolt). *Rai Babu* is a stubborn revolutionary. If he wants to stay here, how can we leave the widowed old man behind? My mother and aunts were unhappy but couldn't reply anything to him. They showered their frustration and anger on my father and uncles, which increased daily. The father and son spoke to each other indirectly. All the older people in the world are stubborn, and their sons are obstinate. It wasn't only happening in our family- the same scene prevailed with other larger families in the camp.

One day, a group of government officials visited us. *BDO, Tehsildar, Bailiff,* and four to five people who measure the land. The *Tehsildar* said, 'At least one family member came with us to the forest. The land will be allotted in your name.'

Refugees will get the land and the house- Will you stay in this old-fashioned house, or will you go to your own home with the family? People in the camp were happy. Grandfather was around and said- 'Didn't I say that *Indira* will make all the arrangements?' They all went to the forest with the government officials- we will see our home, orchards, and rice fields!

But what is this land? We fell from the sky. We were disheartened. It was a deep, marshy forest. Trees like *Bani, Kerua, Gua, Sishumar, Sundari, Swasamula,* and thorny bushes grew on the banks of the river. Will the houses be constructed in this deep forest? Will there be farming on this land? The government officials started measuring the land and noting it down. They allotted one acre of land per family. They calculated fifty *dismils* for the children below twelve years per family and distributed the land among the nine families. They demarcated the land with flags for each family, got their signatures on the papers, and left.

By the evening, Grandfather was very elated; he addressed the people in the camp: ' We got the land because of *Indira*. Our signature and thumb impression is now noted in the official papers of this country. Don't we belong to this country now?'

Grandfather went one step further and gave a proposal - 'Today you aren't going to cook at home. We will cook together as one family and have our food. It doesn't matter whether you have come from *Gopalgunj* or *Thakur* village. Today, all of us belong to *Jambu*.'

Though people were happy, they said- 'the government didn't tell us about constructing the houses; only gave us acres of marshy land with many poisonous snakes and other insects.' During the typical feast, Grandfather could sense people's mindset and said- 'after the dawn, go to your respective lands. Whatever land is required for constructing the house, clear that much of the land, and after that, we will find a way out to build the homes.'

In the morning, Grandfather made his sons and nephew to wake up. Others in the camp reached out to listen to Grandfather's idea. Grandfather said, -whether man or woman of the house, give the responsibility of minor children to elder children, take the chopping axe, hatchet, sickle, shovel, spade or whatever is available with you, and come to the forest.'

The camp people had breakfast and went to their respective lands, and Grandfather followed them. Grandfather sat leaning on a tree with his radio, and people started clearing the forest to build their houses. Grandfather slept and dreamt- *Rai Babu* has become the President of *Jambu* and is flying to West Pakistan in an aeroplane. He has brought the hacked head of *Yahiya Khan* and returned to *Jambu*. When the people finished clearing the land and started returning back, Grandfather woke up and told them about his dream. Listening to him, all of them had a hearty laugh.

On one side, a few refugees like us were busy cleaning the marshy land to create their homes. On the other side, *Indira* was discussing our issues with other countries. At that time, the United States Secretary of State Kissinger was visiting India. Grandfather heard it on his radio.

According to the news on the radio, there was a critical discussion between *Indira* and Kissinger. In the meeting, she included the Army chief *Manekshaw*, and *Indira* said to Kissinger very firmly – 'It's better if you make the President of your country, Mr Nixon, understand that the condition of East Pakistan is terrible and the refugees are pouring into India. It's difficult for India to take care of the situation. We can't withstand this silently because our country will suffer. We have to stop the devastation caused in East Pakistan. If Nixon and the government of the United States of America cannot control the situation,' I will be forced to ask army chief *Manekshaw* to take necessary steps.'

Kissinger was shocked to hear *Indira's* firm statement. On the other side, *Indira* had a closed-door meeting with the President of the Soviet Union, *Mr. Mikhail Yashnov*. A treaty for Peace and Cooperation was signed between the two countries that specified mutual strategic cooperation, and with this, *Indira* made the Pakistan government understand that though they had the support of America and China, India had the help of the Soviet Union of Russia. Let the government of the United States of America remain silent. *Mukti Bahini's* slogan was on the *Hind-Russia* brotherhood, and they have intensified their guerrilla warfare. Being scared, *Yahiya Khan* warned India to withdraw its guerrilla soldiers of *Mukti Bahini* from East Pakistan; otherwise, Pakistan would attack in a couple of weeks. Grandfather said – 'no one knows what will happen in the future, but before anything else, it will be better for us to build our house and settle down quickly in this country.'

People were enthusiastic about constructing their own houses on the land provided to them. The camp was empty during the daytime as they made the necessary arrangements for cooking near the land and utilized time for clearing the land and constructing their houses. Grandfather suggested- 'Before construction begins, everyone here should dig a pond for their family. All nine families should dig nine ponds before constructing their houses. They can use the mud dug from the pond to construct houses with strong walls as *Jambu* is prone to cyclones and floods, so it's unnecessary to construct high walls. After the walls are constructed, they should be covered with a frame of wood and then thatched with palm tree leaves. The dug ponds will provide mud for constructing the houses and fish for food as *Bengalis* are fond of fish and rice.'

Under Grandfather's supervision, people in the camp built their houses, decorated them beautifully, and, upon return to the camp, cleaned the lamp glass for the nights. Some tried to develop a small kitchen garden in their allotted place and sowed mustard seeds. There was brotherhood, love, and affection among the people. They stayed like a family, and food items were exchanged between them. In the meantime, they could hear the sound of the aeroplanes flying above with booming sounds. As soon as the ladies of the house listened to the sound of the aircraft, they immediately took their children inside the house from the playgrounds. The older men were apprehensive that if there was a war, they would drop bombs.

Still, Grandfather encouraged them to be courageous and said-'*Mukti Bahini* of East Pakistan is marching towards victory. It is conquering place after place. *Yahiya Khan* can never stop *Mukti Bahini* from achieving its goal. There is a bombardment on the border of India. *Indira* is also not sitting quietly. Let's wait and watch. All warships and fighter aeroplanes have started their warfare practice. Let's not be scared looking at the military craft of the country flying above its own. If there is a war, then it will be on the border or in big cities. The war will have no effect on *Jambuloka*. Let *Indira* make fighter planes to practice here, and let us clear the forest to make clean land for utilizing it.'

Whatever *Rai Babu* said was followed by everyone, and people engaged themselves with their land development. They started clearing the forest parcel behind their houses and levelled the land.

Grandfather said,' Clear only that much of forest which is required for your house as per your quota.' People thought of farming the land and growing rice, so they worked hard to prepare the ground for cultivation. Grandfather was happy to see them working with a positive attitude. He came to know that *Bholanath Mondal* was blessed with a grandson. In the morning, Grandfather and his grandchildren went to *Mondal's* house.

Mondal's house was crowded as people from other families had come to see the newborn child. One by one, they entered the house and saw the child. They came out and appreciated the plump, pink, and white newborn. *Jambu's* air was filled with the sweet cry of the newborn child. *Bholanath Mondal* met Grandfather in his courtyard and welcomed him. He spread a rug on the courtyard and made Grandfather sit on it. After offering a glass of water, tea, and betel, he started talking to him. He said -We know that our *Mondal* family belonged to *Chattagram, Bholanath* said- we lived there but were tortured. My elder son was newly married to a beautiful girl. During those days, the village *Maulavi* and other miscreants took away my daughter-in-law forcefully from my house. They re-married her to a rowdy Muslim fellow. They made my daughter-in-law eat meat and wear a burka. This newborn child is of my younger daughter-in-law. When we saw the situation of our elder daughter-in-law, we were scared, so we put tattoos on the face of our younger daughter-in-law, shaved her hair, made her wear torn clothes so that she didn't look beautiful, and very carefully left *East Bengal*. As we could settle down in this country, our daughter-in-law is blessed with a child.'

Grandfather was delighted to see *Bholanath's* grandson. He said- 'Mondal, your grandson belongs to yours and all the families living here. He is the first child borne in this place. All the nine families here are no more refugees. When the child takes birth in a country, he belongs to that country. It is his birthplace. Your grandson is the first Hindustani among us. He is the child of *Indira's* land.'

Listening to what Grandfather said, a resolute like *Bholanath* got emotional. It seemed as if Grandfather had a magic wand to make the refugee feel at home. He was the most trusted man for all nine families. Grandfather was very good at counselling people. He moved around the place, narrating the tales from the radio about *Indira* and *Mukti Bahini's* victory. One day in the field, a poisonous thorn pierced Grandfather's feet. Grandfather was in deep pain. All of us ran towards him. My father removed the thorn from Grandfather's feet, but a small piece remained. The place where the thorn pierced through became a sore. All the available remedies were done to cure the sore. Turmeric paste was applied, and medicine and ointment were brought from *Kendrapada*, but the sore couldn't heal. Grandfather was bedridden, but his radio was always with him.

In the evening, few people came to meet Grandfather

after completing their work. Confined to the house, Grandfather counted the number of aeroplanes flying in the sky and how many rocket launchers fell on the border. That day, there was an announcement that *Indira's* speech would be broadcast. People assembled around to listen to the radio. *Indira* said that both countries are trying to interfere in this matter, and those discussing peace are surprised by our decisions and actions. We want to say to those countries – 'India is a peace-loving country, but if war is imposed on us, then we are ready for it.'

After listening to the speech, Grandfather was thoughtful. He said- '*Indira* has told means there will be a war. We all have suffered the consequences of war. In 1965, there was a war between India and Pakistan during the reign of *Lal Bahadur Shastri* of India and *Ayub Khan* of Pakistan. We know the consequences of the war. Let us not worry about the war; instead, we should think about farming as it's time to sow the crops. So engage your sons and nephews on that work.'

While sowing the seeds, people discussed the war, but the children were not scared of the war. They were busy collecting crabs near the *Gobari* bank on the marshy land. People were worried that the subsidized kerosene wouldn't be available without a fight. The cost of rice will increase, and salt will be scarce. Mustard oil will become expensive, and there will be a rise in the overall cost of living.

It was December and frigid. It was almost 11 p.m.; we had already finished our dinner, ready to sleep. Grandfather switched on All India Radio and called us. *Indira* held the cabinet meeting in the evening and discussed with the opposition parties. Listen to what *Indira* is saying in the middle of the night, sitting with the army officials– 'Brothers and sisters of the country! Just a few hours back, the fighter planes of Pakistan bombarded *Amritsar, Pathankot, Srinagar, Uttar Pradesh, Ambala, and Agra*. There is a constant exchange of fire at Punch. All of you know that since March 1971, we have been trying to solve Bangladesh's problems peacefully. East Pakistan was fighting there, and now it has spread to India. India always supported peace. If war is imposed on us forcefully, we are ready for the war. I don't doubt that finally, Indians and Indian soldiers will be victorious.'

-' Extinguish all the lanterns. Grandfather turned down the volume of the radio and said. -'Go and inform all the houses that the war has begun. Delhi is completely in a blackout. At this time, keeping the lights burning is dangerous. Go and inform the people immediately.'

Grandfather's sore feet were in terrible condition, and he couldn't get up from his bed; otherwise, he would have gone out at midnight and informed the people. As Grandfather insisted, two people from our house went out in the darkness to tell other families about the war. The next day, all the refugees present there left their work as they were in fear and sat silently next to *Rai Babu's* bed. There was no more news about *Indira* on the radio. There was only news about *Manekshaw, M.M Nadi, Yahya Khan*, and the war. The war was fought by five lakh Indian soldiers, one lakh seventy-five- thousand guerrillas of *Mukti Bahini*, and three hundred and eighty- five lakh soldiers of Pakistan. There was also news about the bombardment over *Karachi* port and the airports of Pakistan. The navy of both countries was engaged in warfare with the submarines in the Arabian Sea and the *Bay of Bengal*. Gradually, the number of deaths and injuries decreased.

Grandfather heard the news on the radio and

announced- 'Pakistan has surrendered. The war is over in thirteen days. Did you see how *Indira* could become victorious in just a few days? The United Nations has announced East Pakistan as an independent country and has named it as *Bangladesh*. Did you see how things happen? *Muhammad Ali Jinnah* divided the country in the name of religion- Pakistan for Muslims and Hindustan for Hindus. See what has happened in these twenty-four years. *Indira* divided Jinnah's country into two halves.'

There was no other way than nodding the head and listening to *Rai Babu's* political narratives. There was complete silence in the country and *Jambu* after the war. It seemed like the wind had stopped blowing, and the leaves had stopped fluttering. There was happiness in *Bangladesh* after independence but sadness among the refugees. Even after the freedom, the Muslims didn't mend their ways. Still, a long line of refugees wanted to come to India.

We were busy with our fields, growing vegetables, and fish farming. We were busy making money, but Grandfather's sore wasn't healing. There was pus and blood in the sore, and he was in pain, but now people didn't have time to think about him. After the war, people were busy earning their living, so they needed time to listen to the radio news. But whenever they felt that the Indian government was making stricter rules for the refugees, they didn't hesitate to consult Grandfather for his advice.

Once, a group came and asked Grandfather whether to be voting in a few days. The opposition party is saying that if we vote against *Indira* and if they win, they will include our names in the voter list and will issue a ration card in our name.'

Grandfather was listening to them attentively and could make out the games of politicians. He just said a few words, which broke the audience's delusion. He said- I would say one thing. *Indira*, who has permitted us to live in this country, given our land, and saved our lives, let her be in whichever party she wishes, but we will vote for her party.

-We should understand that we are always with her party. Keep this in your mind. We will never be unfaithful- The people pledged. Before they could leave, Grandfather said -'It doesn't matter if any party is promising us to give voter ID, but we will vote only for *Indira*.'

Looking at the condition of Grandfather, people were feeling sad. Still, Grandfathers like *Bhisma Pitamaha* advised them and told them to settle in India safely. That's why people felt a little secure. They started clearing the forest to make it fertile to increase their earnings from farming. As their earnings were good, they bought sarees and toys for their wives and children from *Marsaghai*, visited goddesses *Ramchandi*, and started having fun. They were engaged in different activities to earn more for their family.

In the meantime, they cleared the marshy land and expanded them for cultivation. They planted mango, coconut, and jackfruit trees and reared the cattle. The houses became their territory. They were able to establish themselves in *Jambu*. They were busy with land and cultivation, so they needed more time to track what was happening in the country or the world. There was no one to listen to *Rai Babu's* radio as, by this time, everyone had their own radio. They could listen to *Rabindra Sangeet*, *Bengali* movies, and modern radio songs. The distance between countries was no longer limited because of the radio. People were more inclined towards the songs and plays broadcast on the radio.

Nothing good was heard about Indira on the radio. After the India- Pakistan war, the country was heading towards a socio-economic crisis. There was a revolt in the country against Indira. Indira had burdened the country with two problems- war and a staggering influx of refugees. Indira's *Garibi Hatao* (Eliminate Poverty) slogan helped her win the election, but it gave rise to unemployment. The opposition protested in the parliament, as well as across the nation. Indira made her younger son the President of the Youth Congress, a post in which he gained control over the administration and allegedly interfered in the functioning of the government.

The younger son of Indira used his draconian powers to terrorize and to keep the opposition mum. He added many hooligans and ruffians to the party to silence the opposition. There was chaos throughout the country with road blockage *(Rasta Roko)*, picketing, and *Bharat Bandh*. The opposition leaders like *Jayaprakash Narayan, Morarji Desai, George Fernandez, J.B Kripalani, and Atal Bihari Vajpayee* were arrested. The Congress party leaders tried their best to suppress the dissent. Few Congress leaders compared Indira with the goddess *Durga. Someone like Debakanta Baruah* coined the sycophantic slogan, "India is Indira, and Indira is India." The freedom fighters and the opposition leaders opposed this.

To divert the people's attention from her, Indira instructed the first nuclear bomb testing in Pokhran that could justify her power but failed. There were massive political rallies and mass movements against Indira nationwide. The (Five Principle Program) *Pancha*

Sutri program of Indira's younger son triggered the fire. His influence on Indira and the government increased dramatically, and he had total control over his mother. The battle continued in India, and the condition of Grandfather was deteriorating. Grandfather was unhappy listening to the political unrest and criticism. He stopped speaking to the family members and outsiders. He listened to the news on the radio, and people stopped visiting him. By this time, the refugees were already settled in *Jambu*, so they didn't pay any heed to Grandfather and were busy with their work and life. They no longer required Grandfather's suggestion. Grandfather was confined to his world and the radio.

The radio was playing with a slow sound, but he wasn't listening to the radio and was sleeping. If Grandfather's radio is playing, it means he is doing well. The people in families were busy with their work. On that day, Grandfather had tuned to All India Radio and shouted,' There is darkness all over India.'

-'What happened? What happened? Hearing his screaming, a few people ran towards him. Grandfather had turned insane. He said- 'Why did Indira do this? She declared an emergency in the country.'

We couldn't understand what an emergency was. One of us saw that the sore in Grandfather's foot was in terrible condition. He was breathing slowly as if he was nearing his end.

CHAPTER -2

An old Bangladeshi refugee died. The days of remembering Grandfather and feeling sad also getting over. Still, the journey of countless refugees to Jambu continued.

-Voyage

During April, on the bank of the river *Kabataki*, *Padma Pokhari* villagers were ready with their luggage and gathered at midnight near the boat. It was dark. There was absolute silence as they thought they would be in trouble if there was any noise. But people weren't happy as they had to leave their country. The boatmen were confused as they saw the people carrying so much luggage. They said, 'First, try to save your life and board the boat. If you bring so much baggage, then there is a chance that in the midway, the boat will be drowned.

The heavy luggage and other stuff people were carrying were left behind on the banks of the river *Kabataki*. It's better to escape from this country in the dark. People were boarding the boat to leave the country. The young men were helping the children and old people to climb the boat. He was helping others in this work. At that time, a tall lady with a baby in her arms came into the boat, but her seven-year-old daughter couldn't climb. The mother shouted- 'Climb the boat'. He helped the little girl climb the boat and learned that the child had a fever.

'Unleash the boat: Let's start our journey immediately. There was no time to listen to the other's problems. The light was doused so that the miscreants would not come to know about the boat's movement.

He saw that a woman sitting near to him was crying. Someone was beating his chest, and *Sugen Da's* mother continuously sobbed. Someone sang the national anthem, and others said- 'Our golden Bangla'. A few elderly people were saying- We left our fields. Whatever we went shall be enjoyed by those miscreants.

The boatmen were busy rowing the boat. Wherever the water was deep, they tried to propel it forward with the help of the oars. They were also leaving the country in their boats along with the people of *Padma Pokhari.* On the boat, the family members of the boatmen were sitting quietly. There was only one thing that bothered the boatmen. They wanted to leave this country and reach the other country as soon as possible to save their lives. As it is, the people who lead the life of a boatman are devoid of patriotism. They were only concerned about their earnings and living, irrespective of the country they belonged to. Wherever they go, it will become their own country. Someone shouted- 'Look, we have reached river *Padma.*'

The boatmen started rowing the boat towards river *Padma* as they left the branch of river *Kabataki.* When they entered river *Padma*, a few took the water in their hand and touched it on their forehead. Some said, 'The *Hilsa* fish found in the river *Padma* is delicious.'

Some of them said- 'Can we ever see this river again? They became emotional and bid farewell to *Bangladesh* and river *Padma*'.

It was early morning. The small children were in their mothers' laps, and the mothers were sleeping. The young men in the boat were eagerly waiting for the smog to subside so that they could see a new country. How will the people be; what will be their language and attire in that country? The sky was hardly clear, but where was that new country? They could see only water and water everywhere. The boat was heading towards the sea. It wasn't only his boat moving forward but another five to six boats following them, all loaded with people!

He tried to find out about his family during the daylight. Leaning on each other, his parents were in the boat. At the centre of the boat, the girl he helped climb with folded hands. She had a high temperature. She was closer to her mother, looking around and searching for something. Holding the baby on the lap, her mother was draped in a green saree. She was remorseful. Who are they? Other than the girl, her mother, and the tiny baby, there were no male members along with them. They may belong to someplace other than *Padma Pokhari* village. Perhaps they are leaving the country with the help of any relative from *Padma Pokhari* village. With many apprehensions, he walked towards the girl and stood near her.

He asked the girl in *Bengali*- What is your name?

-Suniti Burman

- And who are there with you?

- My mother and baby brother

- And your father?

- My father is dead!

He heard this and sat down there. The lady removed her veil, looked at him, and again pulled the cover on her face. She was a widow, and what solace could he give these fatherless children? He started talking with the girl to change the topic.

He asked her- 'Where are you going?'

-' We are going to our aunt's house'.

He felt like he had lost his senses, as no one knew where the boat would take them. It will be an unknown land with unknown people. The lives of the people travelling in the boat were confined to *Bangladesh*, *Khulna*, and *Padma Pokahri* villages. Where is the aunt's house of this unknown girl?

He asked her curiously, «Who told you? You are going to your aunt's house?' *Suniti Burman* pointed her finger towards her mother. Her mother said, 'The little girl was asking where we are going, and as there was no other answer with me to convince her, I said to aunt's house.'

He thought for a while. All of them are heading towards an unknown place by giving solace to each other. If the country they belong to is addressed as a mother, then the strange land that will shelter them can be addressed as an aunt's house. The girl pretended as if she had understood everything and nodded her head.

In the meantime, someone distributed biscuits and bread among the children, and the elders ate rice flakes and bananas. Among them, an elderly man said- 'What will we eat and survive before we reach the unknown place as it will take so many days? Eat judiciously and save the eatables.' Others understood the point, so instead of eating more, they ate less to keep some food.

-' Did you eat anything?'

The little girl nodded and said 'NO'.

He took out the mixture packet from his sling bag. On the package, it was written in *Bengali,' Annapurna's* Handmade Mixture'. He liked this brand a lot. He has already left the country, and this mixture packet will soon be over. He said, 'This is *Khulna's* famous mixture, so eat and finish the packet.' The girl was interested in eating but was scared of her mother. Finally, her mother allowed her to eat, which she eagerly awaited. *Sunita Burman* put her hand into the polythene packet, took a handful of the mixture, and ate it as she was hungry.

-' Did you bring any eatables with you?' When the lady was asked this question, she cried loudly. She looked at the tiny baby on her lap and, like an insane person, cried continuously, and She said- 'The small baby has not eaten anything; how can I eat?'

The tiny legs of the small baby could be seen. The baby had turned pale because of the salty wind of the sea. He touched his feet- 'Fever'? The baby didn't have a fever, but his feet were cold. He told the lady- 'Your baby doesn't have a fever; only his feet were cold. Show me his neck and chest. Let me check what has happened to him.' He was startled when he took out the saree with which she was covering the baby. The baby's head was turned towards one side. The eyes were wide open, and there was no heartbeat. When did it happen? Maybe the baby lost his life while travelling in the boat on the river *Padma*. The crazy mother is carrying her child's lifeless body and leaving the country.

She isn't ready to accept that the baby on her lap is no longer alive. She thought the baby had a fever and that he would get well soon if she reached another country. How will he make a mother understand that her baby is dead now? He must have died yesterday, and how long will she carry the dead body of her child? Does anyone know how far the country they are trying to reach is?

He was young and didn't have patience like mature people. He understood that it was no more necessary to console the lady. The need of the hour was to forcibly take the dead child from the mother and to immerse the dead body in the water. He made this clear to all the people who were there in the boat. Slowly, the words spread. Someone in the boat identified the family and said- 'This is *Satish Burman's* family. Oh! *Satish Burman's* son is dead.'

He held his breath. Which *Satish Burman*? Is he the *Satish Burman* of *Khulna*? The person who was well known throughout *Bangladesh*? Everyone knew *Satish Burman's* story, but no one ever saw him. He looked at the family with wide-open eyes. Is it *Satish Burman's* family? Is it so that along with us, along with the people of *Padma Pokhari*, the family of *Satish Burman* is heading in search of a new country? And finally, *Satish Burman's* son died in this vast, lonely sea.

In the meantime, the elderly people in the boat tried to make *Satish Burman's* wife understand so they could take the dead baby from her and immerse her in the water. He moved away from there, slowly through the crowd, and returned to his place. His mother offered him rice flakes, but he couldn't eat. He looked at *Satish Burman's* family: his daughter, who had a fever, and his wife, sitting boldly and sobbing with the dead baby on her lap. He couldn't believe all that was happening around him. He asked *Sukat Mandol,* sitting next to him, "Is she the wife of *Satish Burman?*'

'Yes, yes, she is *Satish Burman's* wife. She doesn't have one of her breasts.'

He couldn't look at the lady sitting there as he felt ashamed. She was there in the boat, covering herself in a saree and pain in her heart. Why would he think that the lady protecting herself, doesn't have one of her breasts? He tried to guess which side of her breast was hacked. By that time, other ladies in the boat had already surrounded her and tried to convince her to give away the dead child for immersion. He could no longer see *Satish Burman's* family as it was crowded.

He could very well envision the past of the people present over there. There was the vast stretch of sea in front of them; there was a country they had left behind and lots of uncertainty about the country they were heading to. The prevailing situation made the lady sit quietly like an owl on a tree. She was scared of the people around her who had evil eyes.

The nuisance of heinous people in *Dhaka* and other villages had created a nightmare. The Bihari tenant Muslims entered the Hindu villages like *jihadis.* They troubled the girls going to school by lifting their frocks from behind and mocking them. After offering prayers, they pelted stones at houses and troubled the Brahmins returning from the temple. They walked naked near the ponds where the village ladies took a bath. They disrupted the celebration of any festival in the village. During the celebration of *Durga Puja* in the town, they would invade the *pandals* and trouble people. They will ask to remove the red flags, or else they won't let you do the puja.' The celebration and joy of the puja burst like a bubble; the puja committee met and analyzed the situation.

The old people were scared and said, let's remove the red flag and put their black flag. Our goddess is already there, the mother of all, and can see everything. She will take care of these demons.'

Those who were middle-aged said- 'If we don't do so, then these demons will pee on our idol and destroy it. There will be bloodshed. It is our puja, and let us do it peacefully.'

The youth in the village didn't have the weapons or the courage. When the red flag is removed, and the black flag is hoisted, those hooligans people leave the place laughing aloud.

These hooligans would reach the place during *Bengali Vaishnava Harihat* with liquor and weapons. They would throw the idols of *Sri Chaitanya and Radha Krishna* on the road. They repeated the same activity during *Manisa Puja, Nagadevi Puja, and Ganga Devi Puja* and spoiled the celebrations. Whenever the villagers got the information of their arrival, they would close the doors of their houses. The people working in the fields ran into the forest, leaving their work behind to save their lives. The shopkeepers would immediately close their shops and desert the place. Mothers would take away their children playing on the streets into the house. Though the ladies stayed indoors, they were too scared of them. If, by chance, anyone comes on their way, there is no way for her to escape. They pointed the sword at ladies, dragged the beautiful ladies towards the bushes, tortured and raped them in broad daylight, and then hacked one of their breasts.

The images of hacking women's breasts were too

scary for the people of *Bangladesh*. In 1947, these ruffians packed the hacked breasts of hundreds of women and sent them to *Sialdah* station in India. From 1947 till 1971, they kept on doing such heinous crimes in Hindu villages. To throw out Hindus from *Bangladesh*, they raped and hacked the breast of Hindu women continuously; because of this, many women suffered and lost their lives. Whoever was alive after being tortured thought that it was better to commit suicide than live the life of a disabled person. The girls who lost one of their breasts became a burden for the family and would hide in the house. They were tortured so much that even the daylight scared them. They feared that the hooligans might cut their other breasts. The parents of these girls were worried as they thought if they left the country, who would marry their daughters with a single breast?

He remembered those old incidents as he looked at the woman sitting with her one breast. When she was a girl at that time, those ruffians had hacked one of her breasts and left her in a pool of blood. Her family members tried to save her life by consulting a doctor. One day, she drank poison, but her life was saved again. People were despised and said -didn't the girl die? Her life is useless as no one will marry her.'

-' Yes, I will marry your daughter. I swear.' There was only one guy in *Bangladesh* who came forward to marry a girl with one breast- He was *Satish Burman*.

I knew *Satish Burman*, a young man in *Mukti Andolan*, had married a girl with only one breast. It's such a big sacrifice. Is there any young man in *Bangladesh* like *Satish Burman*? He was the talk of the town.

Satish Burman became popular among *Bengali* people,

even those who didn't know him or had never heard about him. *Satish Burman* was a part of the country's *Mukti Andolan (Freedom Movement)*. He instigated the *Bengali* people in all the villages by organizing secret meetings, saying we can never leave our motherland in the hands of these heinous bandits. Our Sonar Bangla is now in the hands of the military, orthodox *maulavis*, and heinous Bihari Muslims. This time will pass very soon. Every patriot has to sacrifice. We will offer our blood for our motherland but never leave our homeland.'

We all liked what *Satish Burman* said about the motherland, but the tyranny continued to increase. To save our lives is more important than protecting the homeland, and with this thought, few of us left the country.

During the Language Movement, *Satish Burman* continued with the movement. He said-' They are trying to make Urdu the official language of *Bangladesh*. No one can devoid us from our mother tongue. Will the mother tongue we learn from birth not be taught in schools and colleges? How can *Bengalis* accept this? Our language is our wealth. Many *Bengalis* sacrificed their lives to protect their mother tongue. We will also offer our lives for this.'

People liked what *Satish Burman* said about the mother tongue. The people who attended the meetings, the *maulvi*, and the goons of that village hoisted a black flag on their lands and peed on their orchards and houses. Leaving the language movement behind, they started leaving the country one by one.

Satish Burman gathered the *Bengalis* and gave them information about the changing scenario in *Dhaka*. He consoled the people who were scared about their safety and wanted to leave the country. He said- 'Have patience.' There won't be any more bloodshed in *Bengali* villages as now Yahiya Khan has understood that the villagers are innocent and *Bangladesh* depends on the agriculture and business of these people. The people responsible for the revolt are the well-known professors of *Bangladesh* University, doctors, litterateurs, and bureaucrats. They have now focused on cities, and those who are intellectuals aren't safe now. They have killed *Govind Chandra Dev, Munir Choudhary, Anwar Pasha,* and *Humayun Kabir* of *Bangladesh University*. People like the well-known doctor of *Dhaka, Mohammad Faizal Rubi,* Doctor *Alim Choudhary,* reporter *Nizamuddin Ahamed,* and *Salin Parwani* are dead now. They are killing both Hindus and Muslim intellectuals. We are poor, hardworking villagers, so why will they kill us? Whatever problem has happened is bygone. Now, in *Bangladesh, Hindus and Muslims* are brothers. Our dream is to get independence. Our leader is *Sheikh Mujibur Rahman.'*

We liked what *Satish Burman* said about *Mukti Andolan* and *Sheikh Mujibur Rahman*. But in the rural areas, the small shops were burnt by the monsters, and the legs of the minor children going to school were broken by them. They took the cows from the stables of Hindus, slaughtered them in the village, and prepared Biryani with the meat. In this situation, our liberty and safety were more critical than *Satish Burman's Mukti Andolan*.

When they were preparing to leave the country and save their lives, how could *Satish Burman's* consolation stop them from doing so?

Sometimes, being more patriotic takes the life. *Satish Burman* was also trapped by four of those bandits. Four of them surrounded him and asked-

-' Are you *Satish Burman?'*

-' Yes.'

-'Hindu boy.'

-'Yes'

-'Brave man

-'Yes'

-' You have married the girl whose breast was hacked by us, and you have become a hero, isn't it?

-'It's enough

Satish Burman started answering them boldly. The person who said the motherland belongs to him. The homeland needs sacrifice. The deadly sword of them did that. One of the brave sons of *Bangladesh* was lying dead on its soil. *Satish Burman* was remembered for his sacrifice and was alive through his mythical stories. He had left his family behind. *Satish Burman* was firm in not leaving the country, yet his family was on the same boat to leave the country.

He gazed at the patriot's family after recalling past incidents. The womenfolk in the boat were struggling hard to take away the dead son of *Satish Burman* from his mother's lap. *Satish Burman's* wife was crying bitterly. They could finally take away the dead child and throw his body into the sea. The dead body of *Satish Burman's* son floated on the water for some time like a soft cotton toy and then immersed in the ocean water. The women of *Padma Pokhari* now started taking care of *Satish Burman's* wife. They tied her saree properly and offered her biscuits and water. They gave both mother and daughter anti-malaria medicine and started taking care of them.

He was thinking of something else. He felt as if *Satish*

Burman was still not dead, but his family was destined for another country. Again, his thoughts were *'Satish Burman* was against leaving the country. Did he stay back there? *Satish Burman's* soul is still in *Bangladesh.'*

Of course, *Satish Burman's* ghost wasn't in the boat, but all those in the boat were concerned for his family. *Satish Burman's* wife suffered from malarial fever and was completely shattered as she lost her son. She had a high fever and loose motion. She became senseless and sometimes mumbled like an insane. *Satish Burman's* daughter sat quietly like a statue, looking at her mother's condition. At that time, the boatman pointed to a far distance and shouted- 'We got the country'.

All of them in the boat looked at the forest covered with fog. The boatman who visited this place once or twice said, 'It's India.' The state where *Bengali*s live in West Bengal. The forest which you can see is called *Sundarbans.* From a little distance from here is Howrah Bridge, and then *Kolkata.* We will stay in *Sundarbans.* There won't be any problem if we stay here.'

The boatmen now started rowing with the oars. The boat was getting filled with water because of a few small holes, so few people began removing the water from the boat. Finally, in the evening, the boat reached *Sundarban's Marlakhai.* The shore was muddy, and beyond that was the marshy forest. The place where the boat was set ashore was the land where the people took their first step into a new country.

They were scared of the thieves in this new land, so they lit the lanterns from *Dhaka.* The young people started making a hearth as all of them were hungry. They went around and picked up some dry wood for the fire. The women collected rice and vegetables from each family as per the number of members per family. They started cutting the vegetables and cleaning the rice. When the fire started burning in the hearth, they could see a bit of forest in that light. How far is the human habitation, where is the nearby village, and how will they find a shelter for themselves were the questions in their mind. The people of *Padma Pokhari* left all that old behind and sat together in a line to have food for the first time in a new country.

First, the boatmen, elderly people, and children were served. Suddenly, one of the ladies remembered that *Satish Burman's* family hadn't eaten anything. Someone took a plate of rice and curry and walked quickly towards them. The mother and daughter sat in dim light under a tree in that marshy forest. The lady who took the rice and curry fed the daughter. When she wanted to give food to the mother, she tilted to one side like an earthen statue. The lady screamed with the plate in her hand- she is dead!'

All of them stopped eating.

The fire on the hearth was going down slowly. The food that was left behind was now covered with insects. That day in *Sundarbans Marlakhai*, the cry of the people was no longer heard; one could only hear the sound of the nocturnal birds in the forest and the roar of the orphan daughter of *Satish Burman*.

Sun rose in *Marlakhai*. There was a discussion amongst the heads of the family about the cremation of *Satish Burman's* wife. One of them said he belonged to the *Burman* family. So they are *Kshatriyas*. The cremation will be done by burning the body.' The other one said- 'Where is the dry wood to burn the corpse? Let us bury her.' The ground was dug to bury the dead body. The women present there took care of *Satish Burman's* daughter. None of them ate anything.

It appeared as if *Marlakhai* was a scary place for them. How will they survive here with their family and children? There was a discussion among them- 'Look, there is a marshy forest for miles and miles together. Which fruit will we eat here to survive? Can farming be done in the marshy land?'

-' If people would have been staying nearby, we would have stayed with them in *Marlakhai*. But it's a vast forest. It's inhabited by the Royal Bengal Tiger. It isn't at all safe.'

-' We made a burial ground for dead people in *Marlakhai*. Will human beings stay in this burial ground?' Where will we stay? All of them were worried about it. There was no solution to this problem. The boatmen said,' Let's leave West Bengal and go to *Odisha*. There is a port in *Chandbali* and many people from our country stay there. Let's go and stay there.'

It was something like getting the land and again searching for it. They all boarded the boat to begin the voyage with many apprehensions about the future. *Chandbali! Chandbali!* How is that place? The boatmen told the names of many more spots like *Dhamara, Kendrapada, Mahakalpada, Ramnagar, Batighara, and Jambu.*

It took a lot of effort to remember the names of the places in that state. The boatman proposed – 'Wherever the sun will set, we will get down from the boat on the river bank and cook our food. We will see if there are villages nearby or not. Whether people from our country are there or not? If they are there, then with their help, one or two families will stay back. If we do it in this way, then the government won't come to know about us. If all of us stay in one place in this country, then it will be dangerous for us as they will put all of us in jail or will again send us back to our country.'

All of them were scared after listening to what the boatman was saying and agreed to it. The people from the same village will be separated from each other and will lead an unknown life in a different place. It was tough to digest, but there was no other way. At night, wherever they got down to a plateau from the boat and cooked food, one or two families stayed back there. In the morning, when the boat left, leaving the near and dear ones was more painful than leaving their own country. The family left behind in that place looked at the boat with empty eyes. Similarly, people were dropped in every place wherever the boat halted, and slowly, the number of people on the ship started receding. He thought this country, their village *Padma Pokhari*, is divided into many pieces, each into many countries.'

His mother saw the boat getting empty slowly and asked eagerly- 'Where will we get down?' As a responsible son, he said- 'Wherever we will find a town and shops, we will get down there and stay.'

-' Oh! Do you want to stay in a town? Do you want to keep life like a gentleman? Does your father have money?' His father shouted, and the son and mother duo kept quiet.

His father tried to make them understand. He said- 'We will stay wherever the boatmen will stay. The boatmen must have visited the place for fishing before, so wherever they decide to stay, they must know in detail about that place. If we stay with them, then we are safe. If we face any problem, we can move with them somewhere else.'

Where will these boatmen stay in this country? His mother wanted to know, so she told him to ask them. He got up from where he was sitting, approached the boatmen, and started helping them row the boat. The boat moved forward, and he could gather the information while talking to them. Then he left that place, returned to his parents, and told them the name of a site: *'Jambu'*.

The family started discussing and dreaming about *Jambu*. They thought they would acquire land there, construct a house, and create a business for their living. There was a non-ending discussion between them. They left behind their village, *Padma Pokhari*, dropped people at *Dhamara, Chandbali*, and many other places, and were heading towards their destination. The boatmen rowed in river *Gobari* as the boat headed towards *Jambu*. They said- 'After this turning only lies *Jambu*.'

They all needed rest as they travelled continuously for ten to fifteen days. The boatmen tied the boat to the bank of a river and said get down from the boat. This is *Jambu*.'

As the people in the boat heard the name *Jambu*, they were startled. *Jambu* was a tiny place in this unknown country. How will they survive here in this place? All of them looked at the site with wide-open eyes. It was half-moon night, and few fishing boats were near the river bank. The fishing nets were set in different places; the seawater was entering through it. The fish and dry fish smell was all around in the air. There were a few low thatched houses and a pond at the backside. On one side was the paddy field, and on the other side was the marshy forest land. They finally got a place inhabited by people- *Jambu*.

All of them got down from the boat and sat on the bank of the river as they were tired. One of the boatmen told them about this place- A few people from our country are staying here. I have the address of one of them. His name is *Sukhin Ray*. Let me go and search for him.'

The boatman returned with four to five people. They wore *Doria lungi*, a sleeved vest, and tied the *Pasapalli gamcha of Maedinapur*. They were speaking in *Bengali*. They had left *Bangladesh* long ago and settled here as fishermen. To help the people of his country, one of them pointed his finger at the marshy forest land and said- in this place, there is a vast marshy forest. All of you will clean the forest, construct your houses, and dig the pond. The more you clear the land and make it suitable for cultivation, the more crops you will get. It takes two to three years to get the yield here. First, collect fish and crabs to eat and survive. Till you have built your own house, you will adjust yourself to the families present here. Forget about the past and keep yourself engaged in fishing and catching crabs.'

When discussing their stay at *Jambu*, he suddenly enquired about *Satish Burman's* daughter. Where is she? She isn't seen. He started searching for her among the people who got down in *Jambu*. Four families got down at *Jambu*. *Sambhu Bisaws's* parents, his wife, and their child. *Nimai Sarkar's* family had five members, including children and adults. There were seven members from the family of two boatmen, and he and his parents. Where did the daughter of *Satish Burman* get down? Like her father, she also struggled for life and sat quietly during their voyage. The girl was in the boat when they left West Bengal's *Marlakhai* until they reached *Dhamara*. *Dhamara-Chandbali, Gupti, Rajnagar, Patamundai, Marshaghai, Batighara*. Where did she get down, and along with whom?

He cursed himself. He was busy thinking about

his survival and couldn't know where the girl got down. He could have kept her with his own family. He could have taken care of her. Why couldn't it happen? He was restless and asked one of the boatmen- 'Brother, do you know where *Satish Burman's* daughter got down after her mother's death and went along with whom?' At that time, the boatman was busy arranging his stay with the help of the people at *Jambu*. He was annoyed and said- Try to understand; we are refugees in this country. We have to think about our survival. Why unnecessarily bother about others?'

He couldn't forget the incidents. He caught hold of the hands of *Satish Burman's* daughter, *Suniti Burman*, to board at the end of the voyage? Losing a person from his own country in a new country forever remained a never-ending pain within. While leaving the country, there was only fear but no tears, but now he has only tears in his eyes in this new land.

CHAPTER-3

There was no news whether Satish Burman's daughter Suniti Burman is alive in this country or is dead because of ill health. There was no news about her. In the newly growing village, as the girls attained puberty, some of them were lured to demonic marriages.

During the winter in *Jambu*, with a long antenna, one can see all the *Bangladeshi* channels clearly on television. It is more enjoyable during the daytime, like a mirror.

A serial, *'Kalaratri'*, was broadcast on television during the *Bangladesh* war. It depicted the bloodshed and the indifferences between the Hindus and Muslims at that time in *Bangladesh*. When she remembers that serial, her eyes fill with tears.

Sometimes, she cries in loneliness, but nowadays, it has come down. Many of them say that she cries for petty, trivial things. When she was only eleven, she was married to *Hiran*. *Hiran* was older by three to four years, so the marriage was performed without any knowledge of what a marriage is. There was fear of the police and the magistrate. It was a challenge to perform child marriage in *Jambu, Baulakani, and Ramnagar* areas. Still, the practice of child marriage was going on, and she was married to *Hiran*.

Hiran is the son of *Devakar's* uncle, who lives in the same place, so she addresses *Hiran as Hiran Da* but has never spoken to him one-on-one. But she knows about him and has seen him from a distance. She feels shy when she thinks that *Hiran Da* is her groom. *Hiran* studied till class three in the District *(Zilla)* School. He didn't continue schooling after that and started fishing. *Hiran Da* began the fishing business at thirteen or fourteen and could build his business in *Jambu*. She was waiting to attain puberty and stayed at her parent's house. She could only move to her in-law's house after she reached puberty. Her friends and sister-in-law told her that her conjugal life would start after she got puberty. Sometimes, she thinks that *Hiran Da* isn't a very good person. Is money everything in life? Her choice isn't *Hiran Da*.

Often, she discusses this matter with her mother. Her mother tells her to keep quiet. Sometimes, her mother shouts at her and says- you are already married to *Hiran*. He is your husband. You have the same relationship with him as I have with your father. You have never been friendly with *Hiran*, so how do you know that *Hiran* isn't a nice person? Don't listen to what others say, and keep quiet. Only ever speak like this once you go to your in-law's place. He belongs to the *Mondal* family, and they are wealthy people. If they come to know about this from somewhere, then your father-in-law, *Divakar Mondal*, a straightforward guy, won't take you into their house. You are already married, but if they get their son remarried to someone else, who will marry you? You will stay in this house forever and create trouble for us. You will create problems for yourself. Your younger brother will also be in trouble, and his life will be spoiled.'

She was terrified after listening to her mother.

Post-marriage, *Hiran* kept an eye on her and was vigilant. He would send some gifts to her through her uncle's daughter, but *Hiran* isn't a good person- this notion was already created in her mind. She tried to avoid this thought but still couldn't accept *Hiran*. She was grown up enough to attain puberty, and that's when her distant aunt's son, *Sukumar Da*, came to her house. Whenever *Sukumar Da* comes, there is a celebration in the place. His business was to supply fish and crabs. It seemed as if the people living in *Ramnagar, Baulakani, Jambu, and Batighara* had turned into fish and crab along with their business.

If a boy can catch two giant crabs, he sells them in terms of count and earns pocket money. *Sukumar Da* purchases the crabs from here, packs them, and sends them to *Kolkata*. He would stay in their house for a couple of days during his visit. He was busy with his business during the day, and she was engaged in the kitchen in the evening. She was learning to cook various dishes before departing for her in-law's place. Sometimes, her mother, who mainly lies down on the veranda, gives her instructions regarding cooking and managing household things.

Sukumar Da would sit near the fire to apply oil to his cracked feet and ask her,' Is it so that you got married to *Divakar Mandol's* son?' She nodded her head. He said- you are in this house for a few days then. I know how well you cook, and you will make your in-laws happy, but do you know how to make *Hiran* happy?' She felt a little shy listening to *Sukumar Da*. She thought, 'Doesn't *Sukumar Da* know that in *Jambu*, they know everything by the time the girls are ten?

Sukumar Da has got two chidren. One is studying in class two, and the other is a tiny baby. *Dada* very fondly told her- 'You are a girl. You don't know many things.'

Saying this, he pulled her towards him. He explained to her one or two techniques to keep *Hiran* happy and touched her private part. The next day, he took the crabs and left *Jambu*. After a week, she got puberty, and family members began preparing to send her to her in-laws' place. Sometimes, she would hide and listen to what her parents were saying. Her father told her mother- In our *East Bengal*, I gave gold to your family and got married, but in this country, we have to give gold to the groom.' She could hear a deep breath from her father.

He said- 'Wherever you go, you behave accordingly.'

Before the girl departs her in-law's house, she should visit all her relatives' houses. Due to this ritual, she went to *Sukumar Da's* village, *Batighara*. She cried a lot in front of *Sukumar Da*, and he consoled her. He could sense a thing and said- '*Hiran* isn't your choice. I can understand. Will you go to *Jhansi*? You will live in *Jhansi* like a queen. There is no comparison between *Jhansi* and this rotten place, *Jambu*. In *Jhansi*, there will be servants for you to do your work, and you will have a lot of money and jewellery. Will you marry there? You will get a groom like a prince. If you agree, then I will discuss this with Uncle.'

She thought that *Sukumar Da* is too good. He thinks about her welfare and understands her feelings. She felt cosy about *Sukumar Da*. She said- if you so wish, first speak to my mother. My mother will make my father agree to your proposal.'

Sukumar Da could comprehend everything as she gave her consent. He said I would discuss the matter with the uncle if the aunt managed it properly. You be ready to go to *Jhansi*. Before leaving for *Divakar Mandol's* house, I must send you to *Jhansi*.'

-' *Dada*, I am scared.'

- You are stupid. Why are you afraid? In our *Batighara* area, a girl like you, whose name was *Mamuni*, her uncle and brother-in-law, took her and got her married there. Many girls from our side are married in *Mathura, Kurukshetra, and Jhansi*. They are the daughters-in-law of wealthy families. Now, you decide how you want to lead your life. It's your life, so you have to choose. *Sukumar Da's* sweet words were as if from her dreams. She agreed, but if her mother can understand things, then it will be good.

Sukumar Da tried to convince his aunt with his sweet words, and in turn, the aunt went and spoke to her husband. She knew that her mother dominated her father. Still, convincing others regarding your decision takes more effort, but her mother has the art to convince others.

When uncle and aunt wanted to know in detail about this matter, *Sukumar* said, ' *Narayan Nanda* of this place is the man who initiates this matter, and the groom's family will also pay a lot of money as they are very wealthy. As the brides aren't available for marriage in their area, they are getting their sons married to innocent girls from our area so they can take good care of the family and property. We needn't worry about the marriage, as *Narayan Nanda* will make all the necessary arrangements. *Narayan Nanda* will take all three of you by train to that place and provide you with food and a place to stay. He will show you the groom and their house. If you like, the marriage will be performed in *Sidhi Vinayak* temple, and marriage registration will be done legally. There will be a fourth night and a celebration on the eighth day. You will see your daughter happy in her in-law's house and return. Which parent doesn't want her daughter to be happy?'

She was hiding and listening to the conversation. *Sukumar Da* tried to convince her parents, but her father was hesitant. He said, how will it happen?' My daughter is already married to *Divakar Mandol's* son, and everyone here knows about it. I can't change this decision.'

She understood that nothing could happen now. Her life will be wasted in *Jambu* as she didn't like her groom. She cried, and her mother noticed it. Her mother was already aware that she didn't like *Hiran*. So she immediately burst out to her husband, saying -she had a child marriage, but do you think that time continues? The union with *Hiran* was just like a child's play. Where is it mentioned in any legal paper? If we do anything for our daughter's happiness, it's not unrighteous.'

-*Sukumar*, you inform *Narayan Nanda* and make all the necessary arrangements for us to go to *Jhansi*. It would be good if you could accompany us as this would greatly support us.

She told her husband- 'If you say 'Yes', we will give her marriage there. Don't delay, as our daughter has already attained puberty. *Mandol's* family may send us a message anytime. After that, it will be difficult for us to do anything else.'

Her father kept quiet as her mother shouted at him. While returning, *Sukumar Da* kissed her. She feared whether *Hiran Da* would come to know about this matter. If he comes to know, then he will never leave his bride to get married to someone else. What will happen if he forcibly takes her to his house? Who will stop *Hiran* in *Jambu*? *Hiran* will create a problem and will fight. Slowly, the word will spread in the village, there will be a meeting in the village, and they will throw them out of their community. Maybe the rivals will take this issue to the police station. *Sukumar Da* also warned them about these risks before he left. He said- 'Before going to *Jhansi*, be careful. No one else other than you three should know on this matter.'

One day in the evening, *Sukamar Da* arrived at her house. He showed her the train tickets and said- you will go to *Jhansi*'.

When she heard *Jhansi*, she was nervous. *Sukumar Da* said- 'One of *Narayan Nanda's* trustworthy people will accompany us. He will show us the groom's house in *Jhansi*, make all the necessary arrangements for the marriage, and return with us again.'

They left the village like thieves. Early in the morning, when it was still dark and the area was covered with fog, three left the house and sat in the boat. Still, her father wasn't convinced. He was thinking- our daughter will stay happily in the distant land in a wealthy family?' Her mother was thinking- 'Our daughter will be the daughter-in-law of a wealthy family and will help her parents when they are in need.' She thought, 'She will be free from the dirty, stinking land of *Jambu* and will live in luxury.' She dreamt about the marble house and the handsome groom as seen in the television serial. After crossing the wharf by boat, they boarded a bus to *Cuttack*. From *Baulakani*, *Narayan Nanda's* trustworthy person boarded the bus. The mediator's name was *Chaitanya Da*, dressed in saffron clothes like a saint. On the train, they had a good time. *Chaitanya Da* sang songs and entertained everyone in the compartment, and passengers travelling there became his fans.

When she returned from the washroom on the train, *Sukumar Da* stood outside the door, his eyes filled with tears. He said –you will go away now; will I feel good? I won't go to *Jambu* anymore.' She stopped near the door. On one side of the door was *Sukumar Da*, and on the other side was she. She became emotional. The situation made her think about getting down to the next station along with *Sukumar Da* and running away with *Sukumar Da* to an unknown place. The idea of *Sukumar Da*, *Jhansi*, and the marriage troubled her. She was ready to elope with *Sukumar Da* as she thought he would suit her better. She remembered Sukumar Da's first touch. Also, she believed that the groom in *Jhansi* needed to be better than *Sukumar Da*. Can the groom in *Jhansi* be like *Sukumar Da*? Maybe he has money, but no one has what *Sukumar Da* has.

Sukumar Da- Please, save me. She came and leaned on *Sukumar Da* and said, "Please take me to *Batighara* along with you. I will stay with your wife and children. If they disagree, keep me in another house in *Batighara*; otherwise, take me to *Kolkata and* arrange a rented house. You will come to *Kolkata* via *Kendrapada* by bus and look after your business in *Kolkata*. You will stay with me in *Kolkata* during that time, and I will stay with you happily. There won't be any problem for me.'

She was struck by the cupid arrow. *Sukumar Da* said- 'It's not possible.'

-'Why is it not possible?' She retaliated.

Sukumar Da told her the truth. He said- *Narayan Nanda* will not pardon us if we elope like this and marry. He has a vast network.'

She needed to learn what network meant. She tried to infer the meaning from what *Sukumar Da* said and understood that *Narayan Nanda* wasn't a good person. He is a goon. She thought about *Narayan Nanda* and severed in fear. *Sukumar Da's* eyes were filled with tears. This love story would have continued for some time, but *Chaitanya Da* shouted and startled them. He said -the meal was already served. Come and eat it; otherwise, it will become cold.'

Both of them returned back to their seats. *Chaitanya Da* was having his meal, and she recalled the discussion about the network at that time. She felt as if *Chaitnaya Da* is not what he pretends to be. Where is she going? Where are they taking her? She was petrified. She looked at all the men present in the compartment very carefully. Her father sat beside her mother, and *Chaitanya Da* and *Sukumar Da* were there. She thought that if *Sukumar Da* knew this network was a business, would he work for *Narayan Nanda*? She has to see what that man of *Jhansi* is like with whom his marriage is fixed. By this time, the villagers must have learned they weren't there. They must be gossiping and thinking they have left for another groom. What will Hiran be doing now after listening to the gossip? The train stopped at a station when she was still in her thoughts.

Chaitanya Da said- 'Here is *Jhansi*'.

It seemed as if *Chaitanya Da* knew about everything there. He arranged a taxi, and the cab dropped them in the lodging. There were two rooms in the lodge. One space was occupied by mother and daughter, and the other by her father and *Sukumar Da. Chaitanya Da* didn't stay in the lodging and visited with the groom's family and managed everything from there. The room in the accommodation needed better ventilated, the old television was making terrible sounds, and the toilet was also dirty. *Chaitanya Da* had cautioned them not to venture out and stay confined in the lodge.

She had very little time at her disposal and would be away from her mother. She slept beside her mother, keeping her legs on her as she did in childhood. Her mother tried to make her understand: You will be the daughter-in-law of a wealthy family, so remember to behave that way. Other than your husband, ignore all other family members. Keep all the keys with you. You are the queen, and your husband is the king.

Always remember what I said.'

Chaitanya Da took her parents and *Sukumar Da* to show them her groom's house. When they returned, by looking at their face, she could make out that to whom she was going to get married was really good.

At night, her mother said- 'They have a double-storied building. He doesn't stay with his parents and siblings. His brothers and sisters are married and are staying in different places. The groom's father has a clothes store in *Surat,* so they don't stay here; only her groom stays there. There are many servants, and he has two cars. The marriage will be performed the next morning in the nearby temple pavilion. They are insisting on immediate engagement and marriage.'

-'What about your son-in-law? When she asked her-mother, she fumbled and said –'Don't ask about him. His name is *Jubuli Babu*. If it's fate, then only you get a husband like him! When we reached the place, *Chaitanya Da* was already there. *Jubuli Babu* gave your father thirty thousand rupees and said something in *Hindi*. Your father gave the money into my hand and said –'The son-in-law has said to build a house in *Jambu* with the money. If required, he will send more money.' In our place, we buy the groom by giving money, but is it so that here they buy the bride by giving money?'

There were thousands of questions running in her mind.

Her mother said- you got a prince as your husband. There is a hell and heaven difference between *Hiran* of *Jambu* and *Jhansi's Jubuli Babu*.'

She wondered- 'What's the distance between hell and heaven?' She couldn't calculate the distance and kept quiet. Her mother started counting the notes one by one and said- he had given this money with much love. We will have a good house, and when both of you come from *Jhansi* to *Jambu*, you will stay there.'

She was anxious, whereas her mother was happy with her dreams. There was no sign of *Sukumar Da*, and hardly she could meet her father. A calling bell was in the room, and whatever they required was provided as soon as they pressed it. *Chaitanya Da* had already informed the lodging owner that *Jubuli Babu* would pay the bill for their accommodation and food. 'How is that *Jubuli Babu*? How does he look? Neither the in-laws have seen her, nor has she seen anyone from her in-law's house. Surprisingly, she is going to get married the following day.

She was sitting there as a bride in her veil. Around her were her parents, *Sukumar Da*, *Chaitanya Da*, and a few unknown people. The *Brahmin* chanted the mantras and performed all the rituals of the marriage. She could remember her wedding with *Hiran* during her childhood days. She thought- 'Is this my second marriage?' It was beyond her control to escape from this marriage. *Chaitanya Da* showed her father four train tickets and said- all the rituals are over now. The girl will go to her in-law's place. If we stay here long, the groom has to spend more on us. Will it be good if the new son-in-law spends so much money on us? We will go back to *Odisha* by train tonight.'

Her parents, *Sukumar Da* and *Chaitanya Da*, advised her to live happily in *Jhansi*, and they returned to *Jambu*. She thought- She can never go back to *Jambu* again? How far is her in-law's house in *Jhansi* from *Jambu*?' When she was going to her in-law's place with her husband, she remembered *Jambu at that moment.*

The car stopped near her in-law's house. There were many guests the day she married, but only a servant was there. *Jubuli Babu* had changed his attire and was talking to someone very loudly over the phone, and after a while, he again changed his clothes and went out. *Jubuli Babu* was a very busy person. He was elder than *Sukumar Da*. How can *Sukumar Da* select a person like him for her? How can her mother say this fat guy is handsome? At night, the servant took her to the bedroom in the upstairs. The servant had hung two to three *Rajanigandha* strings on the bed support. He also kept the fruits, *rabdi*, and *Banarasi* beetle for her to eat, but she didn't eat anything. There were so many questions in her mind!

She was thinking, what type of in-law's house is

this? Where are the people who were present during the marriage? Did her in-laws also forget that their son is getting married and the new bride will come to the house? How strange are these people? Do the people in unknown places behave in this way? She felt as if the most unknown person to her was her husband, to whom she got married. Only her busy, middle-aged husband and the servant were in the house. The house looked empty. She felt as if she had been trapped. She is going to get crushed. She was feeling restless.

It was around 10 p.m. in the night when *Jubuli Babu* came to the room and closed the door. She sat still on the bed with her veil as seen on the television and waited eagerly for *Jubuli Babu* to come near her. But *Jubuli Babu* opened the glass cupboard, took out a half-empty bottle, poured the liquor into two glasses, kept the glass near her mouth, and said- "Have it.' She exited the bed, ran towards the wall, and cried loudly. *Jubuli Babu* didn't come near her to calm her down. He sat on the sofa, drank liquor, and talked in *Hindi*. She wasn't able to understand the language. In this situation, other than crying, is there any other option for her?

Her husband approached her, held her head, and made her sit down and shouted, 'Keep quiet!'. She kept quiet and sat down, and then her drunkard, middle-aged husband laid her down on the bed. She tried to defend herself, but *Jubuli Babu* raped her. She was in pain and tears. At that time, she remembered the serial on the television– '*Kalaratri*'. She felt it was not her wedding night but *Kalaratri* (*The Dark Night*).

The man finally quenched his thirst and lay lifeless like a dead mouse on the bed. His mouth was open, and the mosquitoes wandered around it. Let these mosquitoes suck his blood as much as possible. She was now annoyed with herself- He didn't speak to her, didn't show his love to her, didn't cooperate with her, but suddenly pounced on her like a hungry tiger, quenched his thirst, and finally got exhausted and slept like a goat. Can he be called a husband? How could my mother say that he is a prince? How did *Sukumar Da* convince her parents to leave her in this hell?

She cried loudly, and the empty house was filled with her cry. Her drunkard husband shouted, -'Keep quiet and take rest.'

She got off the bed and slept on the marble flooring. It was almost 4 a.m., and she fell asleep. The servant woke her in the morning and gave her tea. She looked at the bed but couldn't find *Jubuli Babu* there. The servant said- he has already left for work and will return at night.' She could understand a little what the servant was speaking in a mixed language of English, Bihari-type *Hindi*, and *Bengali*. Slowly, they could understand each other's language. The servant cooked the food, served it, and cared for her. Sometimes, he would speak to her like a friend, but he kept quiet whenever she asked about *Jubuli Babu*. Sometimes, she cursed the servant – 'Rascal, owner's faithful dog.'

How many more days will it take to understand the person to whom she got married? How many more nights does she have to spend with this drunkard rascal? The servant serves his food in the bedroom; he eats there, satisfies his lust, and sleeps like a goat.

After conversing with the servant in mixed *Hindi* and *Bengali*, she slowly could understand a few things about *Jubuli Babu*. He was trying to help her get rid of the sadness. She wondered how *Jubuli Babu* would help her get rid of her sorrow. How can she trust this man? She can never trust him…

One day, when *Jubuli Babu* was not in the house, the servant cooked non-vegetarian food. A few guests were to visit the house that day, so the servant finished his job quickly. At noon, a few people arrived at the house, along with *Jubuli Babu*. All of them drank soft drinks with the straw. In the kitchen, the servant was frying fish.

She was listening to what they were saying in *Hindi*. She could make out what they were discussing. One of them asked- 'Is the girl fresh?' *Jubuli Babu* said, "Fresh. She is a *Bangladeshi*.' She heard this and shook in fear. *Jubuli Babu* tried to make her understand one night, saying,' -There will be an end to your sadness.'

He is making some arrangements. Is this the arrangement? After finishing their lunch, the servant brought her to stand before them. They didn't have any questions to ask her, and all the men present there looked at her with lustful eyes.

One of them looked keenly at her and said, 'She is good.' *Jubuli Babu* looked at him happily, winked his eyes, and said- 'She is simple but good.' All of them laughed loudly. She felt as if she was entering into a deep gorge. Jabuli Babu is speaking all these things about his wife to others! Her eyes were filled with tears. She didn't get time to cry as the servant took her to another room to change her saree. He gave her an excellent saree and removed all the jewellery she had been wearing since marriage. He even took out her *mangalsutra*. When she cried loudly at that time, the servant kept his palm on her mouth, tried to make her understand like a mother, and said, "- Whatever *Jubuli*

Babu is doing, he is doing for your good. Whom you will get married and stay with is very wealthy; he has a big family, and whatever you want, you will get there. *Jubuli Babu* has so much work here, so he can't give you time. It would be wise if you got married to *Banthu Babu* and lived with him. He is wealthy and also a fun-loving person. He will understand you.' He told her this brought her to *Banthu Babu's* car.

The car left the city and went to an unknown and lonely place. After the servant had taken out her *mangalsutra,* she was scared. She understood that they projected her as unmarried and made her go with *Banthu Babu.* She got married to *Hiran* Da, then to Jubuli Babu, and now she will get married to *Banthu Babu.* The car halted in a place where there was not a single village.

There was a big palatial building amongst the trees. A massive boundary wall covered the area: coconut trees, paddy fields, two to three tractors, a lorry, and a car. She alighted from the vehicle and saw twenty to twenty-five ladies standing there to meet her. She could make out from their attire that they were workers. Two ladies took her, made her sit in the bedroom on the second floor, and closed the door. It's again like a wedding night. There was no marriage, exchange of garlands, or arrangements to welcome the bride.

After 10 p.m., *Banthu Babu* came to the room. He closed the door from inside, switched off the leading light, lit the blue light, and smiled. What can one understand from this? Maybe again, things will be done with her forcibly. 'Let me look at that rascal properly before he pounces on me.' She said this to herself and looked at him. *Banthu Babu* was wearing a yellow colour silk kurta and a white pyjama. He had a moustache, and his teeth were stained with beetle juice. The teeth weren't the proper size, and the moustache was half-grey. Is he her *Banthu Babu*?

He removed his trousers, wore only Doria briefs, and crawled on the bed like a cockroach. On his forehead was a *tilak*. He pulled her near him and tried to make her understand in *Hindi*. She understood *Mathura* as a perilous place. It isn't allowed to go outside leaving the house.' Then *Banthu Babu* showed his cheek to her to kiss him, but at that time, she was engrossed in her thoughts. She remembered that she had come to *Jhansi* once from *Jambu* and was now in *Mathura*. **How many times will she marry and go to different places**? And her marriage will never end. It seemed to her as if a naughty child was sitting on a rubber doll and playing happily. *Banthu Babu's* efforts were fruitful. He satisfied his lust. She thought- for some time, he wouldn't trouble her.

Banthu Babu, wearing his clothes, opened the door and said, 'Close the door from inside.

-Where did my third husband go on our wedding night, leaving me behind? It was almost three to four days, but *Banthu Babu* didn't come. She learned that she was the fifth wife of *Banthu Babu* in that farmhouse.

His third and fourth wives are also staying, and two of his wives have already died. She saw that there were so many ladies and servants in the house. Though the three wives of *Banthu Babu* stayed in the same place, they never met. The other wives were staying in their rooms along with their servants. Many vegetables loaded in trucks from his farm went to the *Kurukshetra* market. *Banthu Babu* was a devout of Lord Krishna, so he was a vegetarian, and ginger and garlic were also not used for cooking. Other than that, *Janmashtami* was celebrated with pomp and show. She learned that she is the fifth wife of *Banthu Babu*, which is a lie. This is his farmhouse, and his original house is somewhere else.

He has a wife and children, but they don't interfere in *Banthu Babu's* business and farm. She had heard this from the servant *Kaushalya*, who had provided her with food. *Banthu Babu* enjoys being with the wives in the farmhouse, and as they grow old, he leaves them. They work in the farmhouse to earn and live; otherwise, they die, and the death is projected as if they died of some disease.

Kausalya sometimes cries. She said that once upon a time, she came there as *Banthu Babu's* wife. Later, she worked as a labourer on the farm to feed herself and survive. All the female servants now working as labourers were, once upon a time, *Banthu Babu's* wives. After listening to *Kaushalya*, she was scared. She thought- 'How will I escape from here?' She started searching for a way. She has heard that *Banthu Babu's* farmers, labourers, tractors, and truck drivers are all faithful to him and are rowdies. The doors, windows, and the farmhouse gate were open, but she couldn't gather the courage to escape.

She thought- *Banthu Babu* has a good network, but everything is possible. How can she escape unless she gets someone's help? Day by day, the place seemed like hell for her, and so did *Banthu Babu*. She was feeling restless. Finally, her efforts were fruitful. She found someone.

He was five years older than her, worked in the farmhouse as an orderly, and looked after the irrigation in the fields. His name was *Adhar*. He didn't wear the clothes like a servant. He was intelligent and clever. He goes to the city to purchase the necessary items for the house. One day, she found him alone and called him. She took him to a room next to her bedroom. The room was dark and was filled with unused things. She bravely left her fear and modesty behind, leaned on the man's chest, and pretended to cry. He was also lustful, like *Sukumar Da*, *Jubuli Babu*, and *Banthu Babu*. Let him be like a demon; it doesn't matter because he is the only one to get her a train ticket to Cuttack.

He kissed her many times in that room. He licked her body like a dog. They spread a bedmat in that dark room without anyone's notice, and *Adhar* always satisfied his hunger. Whenever she asked about the ticket, he would tell her that all the keys to *Odisha* were booked for a month, and he would try again after fifteen days. In this way, he tried to prolong things. *Adhar* was always looking for opportunities to get her. One day, *Adhar* showed her the dream of marriage. He said - Will I book only one train ticket? Let me arrange some money, and then I will book two train tickets. We will go away from here, get married, and stay together. We will go to our native place, Bihar.'

She wasn't in a condition to accept Adhar's tempting proposal again. When will this marriage farce come to an end? Will she go around India from *Jambu* to *Jhansi*, *Jhansi* to *Mathura*, and *Mathura* to *Bihar*? These demons will be everywhere. If she falls in love with *Adhar*, then it doesn't mean that there will be an end to her misery. Something else might be waiting for her. She is like a broken doll who is the victim of love, marriage, and temptation. She is already broken. How many more times will she die?

At *Jambu*, she has heard that a man whose two wives are dead first marries *a Sahada* tree (*strobilus asper*) and then can remarry for the third time. She has also married three of them and is now in the clutches of this young man. *Adhar* is very faithful to *Banthu Babu*. Will he deceive *Banthu Babu* and will take her from there? Once, *Kausalya* said, 'people who deceive and become the enemy of *Banthu Babu* even their dead bodies are not found.'

Does this man have that much gut to do so? She understood that *Adhar* could never arrange a train ticket for her, nor could he take her away from there and keep her in a safer place. He will only try to satisfy his lust. One day, she removed the bed mat she had spread in that dark room and got up. She boldly told, 'Young man, you will come to me the day you bring the train ticket to Cuttack; otherwise, don't turn up. If you get two train tickets, then *Banthu Babu* will come to know about it, and we both will lose our lives.'

After hearing Banthu's name, Babu, the man was scared. After that, she kept herself away from him and searched for a way to reach *Jambu*. She took the chance and was fearless, thinking she would live or die if she ran away.

It was the day of Krishna *Janmashtami*. There was a celebration in *Mathura*. She, along with a few other ladies from the farm, went to a temple for *darshan*. In that crowd, she could easily make her way and reach the station. She thought that the railway station was a better place for her. She looked at the empty platform and felt scared. *Banthu Babu's* people can easily trace her at the railway station.

With such disturbed thoughts, she started crying. At that moment, she remembered two things- one, her father's country, *Bangladesh*, where the bloodshed was. She has heard from her father that a girl tried to escape into India, but they killed her father, and two to three of them raped that girl. The other thing she remembered was the serial *Kalaratri*, which she watched in *Jambu*. Is the same danger lurking somewhere here? She left the platform hurriedly and walked along the train line in that darkness. To hide from the goons of *Banthu Babu*, she paced fast, finally reached a small settlement, and entered the area immediately. The place looked different. Children were playing, the girls were enjoying themselves, and the young boys wearing jeans were showing off to attract the girls. People were happily enjoying the celebration of *Janmashtami*. When she entered the slum, she was apprehensive- either she would be looted or get a train ticket.

Near the hand pump, the women were around to fetch water. She called one of them and narrated her sad story in that broken *Hindi* and *Bengali* language. She pleaded with the lady to arrange a train ticket to *Odisha*'s Cuttack station. They took her to the President of the settlement's *Mahila Samiti (Women Committee)*. The ladies understood the looming danger following her. They decided to hide her and arrange a train ticket for her return. They covered her face with a veil, kept her hidden in an old woman's house, gave her *chappati (Indian Bread)* and *dal(Lentils)* for dinner and served her fish and rice for the next day's lunch.

After two days, four to five ladies were ready to take her to the station as they quietly walked along the train line towards the station. Among the ladies, she was walking, wrapped in a blanket. They helped her get a ticket and board a train to Cuttack. All of them shouted in that darkness- 'Go away! Go away!' The compartment she climbed was special, and many seats were vacant. She sat down and then took a deep breath. She thought about those ladies who helped her, hid her for two days, and gave her a return train ticket.

Were they angels? Were they cursed, that's why they took birth in that settlement?

The ticket collector came within ten minutes. He said -it wasn't the ticket for this compartment. Get down in the next station and go to the general compartment.

She went into the general compartment and saw that it was overcrowded. When she came by train to *Jhansi* for the first time, she went into a compartment with a provision to sleep. Food was provided, but it took a lot of work for her to stand in the general compartment on her return. If there was a little space anywhere, the passengers were fighting among themselves to sit. After a few stations, she was able to make a place for her to sit. In another station, when the girl sitting near the window got down, she went and sat near the window. If it's fate, then on a train or a bus, one gets the window seat. She sat near the window and smiled, thinking about finally returning home.

She reached *Cuttack* station and felt as if she was now free from all the knots and ties of that golden rope; had swam in the air like a feather and finally reached her destination. *Jambu* is close to Cuttack. She will take the bus from *Cuttack* to *Kendrapada* and then will go *to Jambuknot*. From *Jambuknot*, she will cross the river *Gobari* by boat and reach *Jambu*. She felt as if she would reach *Jambu* in a jiffy. She got into an old passenger bus going towards *Jambu*.

In between, she was thinking-*Jambu* must have changed a lot. What must her first husband, *Hiran* Da, be thinking? Did he get married again? And *Sukumar Da*- He must be busy arranging a girl like her for *Narayan Nanda. Sukumar Da* is a rascal. He also has got two daughters. Can he sell his daughter in *Jhansi*? Let him come to *Jambu* from *Batighara for* his business, and she will pee on his face with which he kissed her. She was ferocious and considered drinking the demon- *Sukumar Da's* blood.

In her imagination, she was remembering her father. He never wanted the daughter to get married in *Jhansi* and her mother- She is a greedy and clever crow.

Her parents will be surprised to see her and start crying after listening to her story. She thought about these and wept on the bus. A lady of her aunt's age said- 'Daughter, are you crying?

- Aunty, I am returning to my father's home after many days. That's why I remembered every bit and cried.

She asked, 'Daughter, where is your in-law's house?'

- 'It's very far.' She tried to hide the truth from the unknown lady. As she was hungry and sleep-deprived-, she felt like vomiting. The lady sitting next to her asked- Are you pregnant? How many months?' She was startled when she heard this from the lady.

- 'No, nothing.' She was surprised. The lady turned her face and sat, but her head started reeling.

- 'Am I pregnant?

She kept her hand on her belly in fear- Whose child is this? Is it of *Jubuli Babu's, Banthu Babu's,* or of the man *Adhar* for whom she laid the trap to get a train ticket? Who is the father of the child? She couldn't comprehend. All the demons sucked her, and now it's the result of that poison that has taken the form of a seed. She got off the bus in *Kendarapada* and boarded a trekker, but one thing troubled her.

She thought- 'Shall I return to *Jambu* or go somewhere else?' She was in a dual mind. But where will she go? Again, how many times she will be passed from one hand to another hand? In between her thoughts, the trekker headed towards *Jambuknot* from *Marshaghai*.

There was no change in *Jambuknot*. The only visible difference is a platform built in between near the Shiva temple on the river bank. The tea stall of the *Maedinpur* uncle was still there with wooden benches. On the other side of the river bank was a boat for *Jambu*. She will feel confident and relaxed when she reaches *Jambu* Ghat from *Jambu*knot. Ten to twelve passengers were waiting for the boat to cross the river. She didn't recognize anyone. Why will they recognize her? She wore a *salwar kameez* when she left *Jambu* for *Jhansi*. Now, she is returning, draping a saree like a *Marwadi* woman with a baby in her womb.

After the boat reached *Jambu Ghat*, she got down and walked quickly towards her house to meet her parents, neighbours, and near and dear ones. Her mother looked at her in surprise, and then she held her and cried. She asked who had come with her, but she couldn't reply. She searched for her father. Her father was paralyzed and was sleeping on the bed. She thought that her father would be a great support to her, but now he wasn't able to speak or hear. He had a cataract in his eyes, and his mouth was open with the saliva dripping from it. She kept her head on his chest and called- 'Baba, I am your daughter.'

The old man's lips shivered, but he couldn't answer anything. She kept her head on her father's chest and cried loudly. Her mother tried to stop her from crying and asked- How come you came alone so far? If you have come here without telling them, will they take you back when they come to know?'

She tried to make her mother remember the past incidents and asked- 'How did you reach *Marsaghai* through *Sundarban* during the war? You saw that it's not possible to survive in *Marshaghai*. Then how did you reach *Jambu* by crossing Chandbali and many other places?' During the war, people found ways to save their lives. Similarly, I have also won many battles in my life. How long is the journey, and what the distance is? I had only one thing in mind: to reach *Jambu* and to stay in my house. Mother, it's my willpower which has helped me to get here.'

She mumbled to herself but didn't utter anything to blame her mother for her plight. How can she unburden her mother, who has already considered her a burden?

Her mother started narrating this side of the story. She said- 'Your brother *Khokan*, who is still not married, has decided on his own to marry a girl, and before marriage, he is giving them his earnings. He goes fishing in his owner's trawler for fifteen days, and when he returns to *Jambu*, he only visits us but returns to stay at his in-law's place. He doesn't even take care of his ailing father and this house. What's the point of having a son?'

Despite being in *Jambu* for almost a week, *she noticed Khokan* didn't come home. Slowly, there were financial issues in the house. She used to live in *Jhansi* and *Mathura*. There was a fan, a good bed to sleep though she was a victim of lust. There was good food and many servants- all these were good. She felt as if she was in darkness at *Jambu*. She thought her family would support her, but the condition of her house wasn't good. Father was a paralyzed patient, brother was carefree, and mother was a careless and lazy lady. After returning to *Jambu*, she couldn't look at her mother's face.

As she stayed in the house, there was always a quarrel between them. Her mother was always angry with her. She thought about her ill fate. Her mother never tried to understand what her daughter had gone through. Instead, she was always bothered about her brother *Khokan*. She was repeatedly handed over like an animal from one person to another. Finally, she returned to her home, but her mother was thinking about how to send her back to that hell. Her mother never wanted her to stay in that house, so she always poked her and asked, "Did you get permission from *Jubuli Babu* to come here? You had been here long, but why are they not searching for you? Did you fight and come here without informing them, or did you stay with someone else and break your family and come here? Did you kick the wealthy family and leave?'

Her mother had thousands of questions like these. Do the witches have ears? Can they listen if anything is told to them? She sometimes thinks in this way. She kept quiet irrespective of her pain, but her mother was never silent; she would often taunt her and ask, "Tell me, what have you done there? You have been staying in *Jambu* for many days; now go to your in-law's place.' There was a limit to tolerating things. She made herself bold enough and told her final decision to her mother.

-I have come to my own house. I have come here forever. I will never go back to that hell again.'

Her mother was startled and said- 'What did you say? Will you stay here for your whole life? Remember that you are carrying others' identities in your womb. For your in-laws, it's precious. You have to go there and give birth and then can come back.'

-' I will take care of my burden.' She said this and went away from there. Her mother always behaved as if she was the head of the house.

She shouted and said –I don't have money to care for

you and your child. Look at your father- he is not capable of doing anything. Your brother is carefree. It's better if you go from where you have come from.'

-' I will give birth to my child here in this house.'

-' How is that possible? Your brother will marry that girl one day and come to this house. Where will my son and daughter-in-law stay? There are only two rooms in the house. In one of the rooms, your father is lying half dead, and in the other room, your younger brother will live with his family. Where is the place for your child in this house?'

-' Is this not my home? This is my father's house.' She said firmly. But it didn't work in front of her mother.'-' If this is your father's house and you want to stay here, ask your father first. Let me see what answer you will get from him. You don't know how hard I worked and how often I went to the ward member to get the house under the Indira Abash Yojana (*Indira Housing Scheme*).'

- There will be only one room in *Indira Awash*. How did you make two rooms? You have made the house from the money that *Jubuli Babu* gave you. This is *Jubuli Babu's* house. I am the owner.' She started thinking aloud. She was already in pain because of the situation that she had gone through. Other than that, her mother is always fighting with her. Both of them behave insanely.

As the mother and daughter quarrelled, a large gathering of neighbours was outside their house. Her mother shouted and screamed.

-'Look at this shameless girl. She is carrying an illegal child in her womb and saying she will stay here. She will stay in this colony. If she stays here, she will spoil all the girls of *Jambu*.'

She burst angrily as her mother spoke of the illegal child in her womb. She narrated the hidden truth about her mother before the people and said- 'Look! She is the mother who has given birth to me. She sold me in *Jhansi* because of money, bought this house with that money, and is now trying to throw me out of the house.'

All the neighbours were enjoying the mother-and-daughter duo and their drama. They were standing there, discussing them and laughing. They knew very well about her tigress mother, innocent father, and younger brother. The only thing was they hadn't seen the daughter for a long time and had only heard different things about the daughter. No one knew the daughter was married, so many people slept with her, and finally, she returned to *Jambu*.

Her mother said to the people who were present there- 'This issue has to be sorted out.'

-' I will sort out the issue now.' She said in a loud voice to all of them present there.

She ran in front of everyone, searching for a room for her to occupy. She will give birth to her baby there. Will she occupy the room where her father was sleeping, which had all the vessels and other household things, or the room where the rice bags and other useless things were stored? There was a bed with a dirty bed sheet and pillow where her brother would come and sleep occasionally. She decided that she would stay in that room. If half of Indira Avaash's house is of her younger brother, then let her parents and brother remain in one room. The other room is for her- Where did she get the strength and courage to fight for her existence? She didn't know? She benefitted from these marriages with the demons, and she got a home at last.

If River *Gobari* continues to exist, there will be fish and crabs. She can work independently and earn her living without depending on others. She could gather her courage. She pulled out the stringed cot and the bed from her brother's room, and put it in the room where her father was sleeping. She lifted four gunny bags filled with rice and kept them on the veranda, kept one bag for herself and then cleaned the room. She felt proud of herself as she could occupy one of the rooms in the house. The neighbours were looking at her in astonishment. *Jambu* was shaking with the scream of her mother.

She stood firmly on the threshold of that room, pointed her finger, and told her -Let me see who dares to throw me out from here.'

She stood firmly in her house.

CHAPTER -4

She was home- she stood firm again in Jambu. Besides the fish and small businesses, a few incidents created ripples. A government notice with a government seal was served to someone in Jambu. All of them are confined by the notice!

Twenty-Eighth December Two Thousand Four. This date will trouble him for a few days, and his mental faculties will not work. He will either become insane or will commit suicide. This was his condition.

Everything seemed unknown to him, including his family members, *Jambu, Jambu's* marshy forest, river *Gobari*, and the *Bay of Bengal*. There was a fear within him. He felt as if he would be squeezed between two countries.

When the notice was served, he was busy in the fishing business near the estuary of river *Gobari* and the sea. He had spread the net during the high tide. The *dinghy* was still in the still waters, but he wasn't alone. Hundreds of sailboats had come for fishing. The fishermen's talks were creating ripples in the water. That was when a boat came towards them from *Jambu* with two foreign tourists on board, and along with them were four to five Indians. They have come to visit *Hukitola*. A person in the boat was from *Jambu*. He shouted and said to one of the fishermen who was known to him that a notice had been served to three hundred and thirty- three people to leave India.

'Is our name in that?'

The two brothers asked each other. The news spread from one sailboat to the other. They asked-'Who has got the name list?' By that time, the boat speeded towards *Hukitola* with the tourists. The boat has already left the place after giving the news. How can he remember so many names? He was terrified, sitting on the *dinghy*. The net in his hand became loose, and the fish on the net again jumped into the water. Both the brothers were disheartened. They heard the other fishermen discussing the notice in other *dingies.* He had the apprehension of his name being on the list. He immediately turned the boat towards *Jambu*.

When he reached *Jalipada* Bank, it was almost dark. He got down from his *dinghy* in that knee-deep muddy water and tied it. He climbed up from the river bank to the elevated place. In the meantime, like lightning, his younger brother ran towards the house. His younger brother is reticent, active, and hard-working during fishing, but he will not be seen around once they reach the bank. The younger brother doesn't understand the responsibility as he is carefree.

He was still standing in that elevated place like a ghost in the prevailing darkness. In front of him was the zig-zag path which leads to his house. A small pond filled with water lettuce was on one side of the road. Over the pond were flying many fireflies. His condition was like an insect that doesn't have its own light. He walked hastily towards his house. There was a hue and cry in the house at midnight.

'What is the notice?' He entered the house and asked immediately if the name was mentioned in the notice?'

His wife and younger brother started crying loudly.

'The notice is in your name.' His wife told him and fainted.

-Go and get water. Sprinkle water on her face. Go and get the water immediately.

He was nervous, and in the meantime, his younger brother brought water and sprinkled it on his sister-in-law's face. She became conscious, looked at him, and was about to cry again. He stopped her from crying.

His wife said –'notice is in your name.' You will leave India in a month. There is no notice in our names. If you leave *Jambu*, how will we live here?' His wife was crying bitterly. The neighbours immediately opened their doors and came outside. Four to five of them came and surrounded him in his courtyard. They wanted to know and asked-'What is the matter?'

Hundreds of notices were served in *Jambu*. In our locality, *Balipada*

Mukul Rai, Bholanath Mondal, Sanatan Biswas, Akul Rai, Ranjan Jhali, Nirmal Mondal, Kartik Mondal, Sambhu Biswas, Panchanan Mondal, Narayan Biswas, Sanath Mondal, Vivash Rai, Kunipada Biswas, Kumar Biswas, Sunil Biswas, Amar Rai and Nimai Sarkar – there are seventeen people on whose names the notice is served to leave India. There is an apprehension that the *Odia* people will take away our goats and chickens after this. They will take away our houses, fields, and other things.

The man who was saying this, his throat was choked,

and he couldn't utter anymore. He started coughing, being scared of the notice and the *Odias*. Others were standing there like a log in the darkness.

I will leave India if required, but let me sleep till the morning. He sent them all away and returned to his bed, exhausted. His wife was still crying when he was yawning. He covered the bed with a mosquito net and took his wife in his arms.

He went to *Nimai Surgen's* house in the morning with the notice. Before him, *Ranjan, Nirmal, Kartik, Sambhu Biswas*, and many more people were there with their notices. *Nimai Surgen* was reading the notice in English, making each of them understand it in *Bengali*. He also waited for his turn to come. The content of every notice was the same. Only the name, father's, or husband's names were written in the notice in *Bengali*; they were disheartened. The notice order tore them apart-

Government of Odisha

Department of Home Affairs

-Directive-

Bhubaneswar, 28/12/2004

By the 1947 Foreign Law, approved by Home Ministry, Government of India, as per section- 31, No 3, Sub-section- 2/ Notice no 413/57(1), dated 19/04/1958; Odisha State Government orders the Bangladeshi citizen so and so, father's name so and so, staying in Kendrapada District to leave India within 30 days of the receipt of this order otherwise necessary steps will be taken legally to extradite them from this country.

The two lines from the notice echoed in his head- *Leave India within a month, otherwise dismemberment.*

He returned home and sat down. He was restless. He thought- 'If I leave India, where will I go? Our home and land have already been occupied by the Muslim people in *Bangladesh*. My name isn't there in the official records of that country. I was born in *Kolkata*. How can I leave India and *Jambu*? How come my wife and younger brother are Indians, and I am not? What type of notice is this?'

Do the insane people of this country write such types of notices? A group of people is now in trouble after reading it. He choked, and his hands became numb. He took a little bit of tobacco and chewed it, and that helped him to gather some. He called his wife and younger brother and said, -'I have to leave India after a month; otherwise, they will take me in the police van and drop me near the border. Maybe I will stay in the refugee camp there. *Bangladesh* government will not accept me, so I will live in the refugee camp until I die. What else?'

He narrated to them everything that was told in the gathering. After listening to him, his wife and younger brother cried bitterly. It wasn't only his house; the cry was heard from other dwellings where the notice was served. There was gloominess all over the atmosphere. In the pain of separation, people stopped cooking, and their relatives from *Batighara*, *Marshaghai*, and *Kedrapada* visited them. The hosts treated the guests well, and there was a discussion about it in between; they were told that a more prominent congregation would be on this matter.

The meeting will be held on the ground next to *Jambu* High School. He had a corn (popularly known as fish corn) on his right foot, so he limped a bit, attended the meeting and sat in the last row of the congregation. The *Sarpanch* of *Jambu*, *Mrutanjaya Mondal*, Block

Chairman *Balram Parida, Lakshmi Haldar, Bipul Pal, Nikuj Sikdar, Milan Debunal,* Batighara's *Sarpanch, Girdhari Giri* were sitting on the dais. On the backside, there was a banner- *Utkal Bangiya Surakhya Samiti*-2004. He sat under the shed of the canopy and listened to the speech.

It was said –' Despite all the differences of opinion, we have made a *samite (council) to* protect our *Bangladeshi* brothers and sisters. The notice that the government has sent is wrong. Three hundred and fifty-three people in *Jambu* are served with the notice. In *Ramnagar,* two hundred and fifty families have been served this notice. We will fight against this notice, and they ought to withdraw it. We will go to *Bhubaneswar, Kendrapada,* and if required, will raise this issue in the Parliament in Delhi. But for this, a lot of money is needed, and if all of you can contribute something, we can fight for you so that you can stay in India.'

- Yes, Yes, we will contribute. We will stay back in India. A few sitting in the front raised their hands out of despair. Per head contribution was decided in the meeting. He could very well guess that. Before he reached home, he heard a few people discussing and cracking jokes about this issue. He was surprised. When people are in trouble and pain, they can't take their food properly, and their family members are crying, how can a few joke about it?

The joke was on his family. They said he was an illegal migrant, and his wife was an Indian. Sujit Mondal of *Jambu* is an illegal migrant, whereas his nine-month-old baby has a birth certificate from India. Strange! In one of the families, three children are illegal migrants, and the mother is Indian. There were many anomalies like this. Lakshmi Mondal is an illegal migrant who has lost her parents, but her husband, *Prafulla Mistry,* is an Indian.

The *Maedinapur Bengali*s were served the notice, and the most fantastic thing is two *Odia* people were also served the notice as *Bangladeshi* illegal migrants. Many people were served the notice in *Jambu, Mahalkalpada, and Kharnasi.* It came to the notice that in a family, few members were served the notice, whereas others were not. The notice divides husband and wife, children, and old people in a family. People will be divided among two countries again. This was undoubtedly a joke, but still, he couldn't digest it. He lost his interest in fishing. In whose name the notice was served, they were all helpless.

His *dinghy*, his net, the hard work of both the brothers-All in vain. He goes fishing ten to twelve days a month, from full moon day to *sashthi*. Sometimes, they get plenty of fish, and sometimes they don't, and other than this, now there is this trouble of the notice. The day passed slowly, and the fishing activity stopped. Money was scarce, so managing the house and purchasing medicine for his pregnant wife was a challenging task for him.

He went to the ration shop and stood in front with his ration card. The dealer checked his name and yelled at him- 'You are an illegal migrant. You will not get the ration.'

He was startled. That means our name has also reached the dealer. He returned home. As the bag was empty, his wife asked-'What happened? Please, tell me what happened.' He was swamped in finding his papers, proof of his stay in the country. He took out an old article from the polythene cover. He got an evidence certificate in which it was mentioned that he was a refugee. It was written in the paper that, first, they were in the *Charbatiya* relief camp, and in 1957, they came to *Jambu*, so they weren't illegal migrants. As they were in the refugee camp, they were refugees.

He took that evidence certificate, ran into one of the members of *Utkal Bangiya Surkshya Samiti,* and showed it to him. The member asked- 'Brother, do you have the refugee certificate? The people of *Jambu, Rajnagar* area who were served the notice among them most have many cards of this country. Whoever is served the notice for them, these cards are invalid.'

He can't vote.

He won't get a ration.

For him, a BPL card is a waste.

He won't get Indira Awas.

No bank will give him a loan.

He won't get any annual pension.

All the cards in his name are invalid.

Surakshya Samiti member counted his fingers and made him understand. Each and every word pierced through his heart. The *Surakshya Samiti* member consoled him and said- 'Brother, our fight is to convert those invalid cards into valid ones. You keep all these papers carefully. It will be useful when required. Give our *Surkhya Samiti's* donation of five hundred rupees, sit at home quietly, and watch what happens. There will be one more notice passed, and all your cards will become valid, and then you can go to the ration shop to get the ration. When you show your card, you can vote. When you go to the bank for a loan, then you will get the loan. It will be only possible when your cards are saved; otherwise, if you are a person without any card, there is no value of yours in this country.'

He was frightened by what the *Surakshya Samiti* member told him: "Tomorrow I will go fishing. There are two more days left for the good day to catch the fish, and then I will give the money.' The committee member said- now you can go. Hundreds of people have already paid the donation. Are you sleeping? We won't tell you so many times. If you wish to stay in this country, arrange the money in three to four days.

He thought he would faint if he stayed further with that *Surakshya Samiti* member repeatedly asking for donations. He quickly returned home. He has to pay the contribution to stay in this country. What can he do to arrange money for that? He can only catch fish, collect crabs, and sell them to earn money.

He finally decided to go fishing. The *Sashti*, which falls after no moon day, would get over in another two days. He knows that the time could be better for fishing. All his hard work will go in vain. He saw that people on whose boats the notice wasn't pasted were doing well in their business, and others were in trouble. People without any work spent their time playing cards. His brother also wore half pants and a vest, played cards, or went to *Jambu's* market in his cycle. Few people have injected this thought into his mind that he isn't an illegal migrant but a refugee, so he was trying to get separated from him. He learned that he frequently visited one of the relatives' houses in *Kholaghat* and is in love with *Rupen Biswas's* daughter. He plans to leave *Jambu* for *Kholaghat* and work in someone's boat as a labourer. He thought if the notice had come in his younger brother's name, he would have stayed with him, but the brother was planning to leave. His eyes were filled with tears when he thought about his Indian brother going away from him because he was now an illegal migrant. However, he called him to go fishing. He said –'Let's go fishing as there is a lot of expenditure in the house.'

He tried to hide the matter related to donations from his younger brother. His brother refused and said - this time, no one is going for fishing. What is the need of wasting oil and doing so much hard work?'

-'It's not about loss and gain. Whatever fish we get, we can sell and manage the house.'

His brother said- 'If there is any problem in managing the house, then I will make necessary arrangements for myself. I will come to the house once every month. To manage the house is my responsibility. Whatever you can do, you may.'

Amidst this chaos, he never thought his brother would get separated. He was in deep pain. His wife could understand him well. She came, hugged him, and told him- Let him go, he wishes. My child and I are there with you. Wherever you go, we will go.'

He had completely forgotten that his wife would deliver a baby. He touched his wife's belly with his hand. He cursed himself and thought of an illegal migrant father and an Indian mother- What will you be, my dear child? Will you also be divided between the two countries?' As a father, this was the first time he spoke so softly to his child in his wife's womb. His wife was happy. She applied lukewarm mustard oil to his feet and arranged his bidi and tobacco. He ate rice and mixed vegetable prawn curry as he was hungry and remembered the *Bengali* song which he heard during his childhood days-'*Jodi Tor Dak Shune Kau Na Aashe Tobe Ekla Chalo Rae*' (If they pay no heed to your call, walk on your own). He took his *dinghy* and went fishing in the river *Gobari*.

He thought if he managed to arrange the money for the donation, he could stay in this country. He took his boat and went for fishing in a haste. He has always been for fishing with others. He slowed down his boat near the *Chataka* and anchored it. He tried to put the fishing net alone and took all the pain to spread it.

Where are the fishes? He could get a few fish and prawns worth hundreds to two hundred rupees. He cursed the day. He sold the fish to another man in a *dinghy* there. He waited patiently for the rising and falling tide to get more fish and crabs. He ought to earn money to donate to the *Surakshya Samiti* to stay in this country. He waited patiently with courage and determination. He lifted the net when the water receded and could gather fish and crabs worth two hundred to two fifty rupees. He felt like the fishes and crabs were playing hide and seek with him as he was in need. He didn't carry any ice, so he sold the fish to the other people in the *dinghy* and returned home; he took out a hundred rupee note, gave them to his wife to have fruits and went to the *Surakhya Samiti* to deposit his donation to *Nikunj Sikdar*. During that time, a meeting was held in *Jambu*. It was announced in the forum that all will be safe and will remain in this country.

A member of *Surakshya Samiti* said that in 1971, there was the *Bangladesh* war. Before that, there were differences between Hindus and Muslims, leading to blood shade. At that time, the Prime Minister of India, Mrs. Indira Gandhi, brought the *Bangladesh*is to India. In the year 1977, *Nalini Mohanty* became the MLA of that area. To get the votes of *Bangladesh*is, they were given a ration card and voter ID card. Later on, it was noticed that *Nalini Mohanty* got fewer *Bangladeshi* votes from *Jambu*, and there was a lot of political pressure. So, in 2004, the list of illegal migrants was made, and the notice was served. The local police, *Tehsildar*, and Revenue Inspector served the notice to the people. In many notices, the place where the name would be written was kept blank, and at that time, few politicians entered the names in the notice and struck off a few names.

Many illegal migrants stayed in *Jambu* but didn't receive the notice. Only selected people who supported Congress party were served the notice. The people from *Mahakalpada, Khansa, Baulakani, Batighara, and Jambu,* who received the notice, have always given their vote to Congress for ages. *Bangladeshi*s will give their lives but never give their votes to anyone other than the Congress to which Indira Gandhi belongs. All the *Bangladeshi*s and refugees support Congress –still, many more troubles ahead.'

What trouble? The people in the gathering asked.

Another speaker stood up and said, «Today, few more people are served the illegal occupation notice. All the refugees supporting the Congress party will get the notice tomorrow. You were there with Congress during your father's time, but in between, many have changed their party, but still, the old files are there. Any time you may be served a notice for an illegal stay. Who can say when one will get such a notice?'

A few old people who were refugees and supported Congress asked,' What will we do now?' At that time, *Lakshmi Haldar* said the people who had received notice had already given the money, and now those who had not received the notice would give the money. Priory, we will get the injunction from the High Court. We will make all the necessary arrangements so that you don't receive the notice in the future.'

There was dead silence in the meeting. After some time, a few refugees raised their hands and said- We will give the money.' He noticed that the primary intention of the meeting was to collect money to provide safety to the refugees. He counted five hundred rupees and gave it immediately. He assumed that his name must have been entered into the *Surakhya* list, so he had no reason to stay back. He left the meeting and returned to his house.

Wherever he sat in *Jambu*, people avoided him as he was branded as an illegal migrant. He noticed that the refugees helped each other in their time of need. Still, the *Bengalis* who belong to *Maedinapur* looked at them differently. They thought these people would go from here, so what is the necessity to stay connected with them? They kept themselves away from illegal migrants and avoided speaking to them appropriately. One day, he met an old childhood friend, *Shovan*, from *the Maedinpur* area near the river banks. Whenever they met earlier, they had a good time together. *Sovan* always teased him-'Sweet tooth *Bengali.*' he called him-'Sour tooth *Bengali.*' Because of this, there is always a difference between *Bangladeshi Bengali* and *Maedinapur Bengali.* But this time, *Sovan* ridiculed him and said, "You are an illegal migrant, and your wife belongs to this country. After you leave, she will stay here alone. She is the wealth of this country.'

He couldn't reply to *Sovan's* ridiculous comment and was angry after hearing about his wife. He said - go away, you *Maedinpur Bengali.* You have a very narrow mind. It's better if you talk less.'

'Are you angry?' *Sovan* Sarkar ran behind him, but he didn't turn back to look at *Sovan*. He wanted to go home but hesitated. His younger brother left *Jambu* after the notice was served. He has left for *Khola* to earn money and is enjoying his life in *Rupen Biswas's* house as he will get married to his daughter. It's time for his wife to deliver the baby, but he can't provide her with an excellent diet. *Angan Badi didi* has given her some iron tablets, but how long will she eat those? She needs good food. He isn't able to catch a good number of fish, and, on the other hand, the notice period to leave the country is now within a month. There are hardly ten more days left. What will happen next? Whatever will happen, let it be. If I have to leave the country, I will not stay hungry; I will eat well and wait for the day. He got up from wherever he was sitting and thought he would not burn the fuel and go so far to *Chataka*. He will spread his fishing net in the river near *Kalipada Ghat*, closer to his home. With whatever he will earn, he will manage the house and the fuel cost for the *dinghy*. He spread his net in the middle of the river and looked around. To his left was *Jambu Ghat*, to the right was *Batighara*, and to it was *Chataka and Hukitola*, but where is the sea? On the other side of the sea, at a distance, is *Bangladesh*, which belongs to his father, but he is now suffering in India. He became emotional and cried loudly while sitting on his *dinghy*. A person in another *dinghy* shouted from a distance- 'What happened? He immediately stopped crying.'

He tied the *dinghy* near the bank of the river and walked towards his house. Two people were standing there, and their topic of discussion was about the notice. He was no longer scared of ghosts as the news was scarier than the ghost. Sometimes, when he feels too much restlessness, he visits *Nimai Surgen*.

Nimai Surgen was a refugee. They were *Surgen* in *Bangladesh* and were under the Scheduled Cast category. Whatever the Brahmins do, *Surgen*s also do the same. They are called *Namasudra*. *Nimai Surgen* is literate; he does his own business and is a little involved in politics. He is a member of *Jalipada* School. He helps those who have received the notice as friends and guides them for benefits. Though *Nimai Surgen* scolded him, he still asked, 'What will happen to the notice? What is the matter?'

Nimai Surgen heard the question and started scolding again- Of all those who received the notice, you were the one who was scared most. You pay heed to those useless leaders, gave five hundred rupees each, and slept peacefully. But now there is a rift between *Utkal Bangiya Samiti*, and it is because of the money that they got from people like you. They aren't working for your safety and will never work for it. They will never go to court. It takes a lot of work to get the job done from Home Department.'

He paused and said- they were showing their cunningness in *Jambu* and *Ramnagar*. They are scared to go to Cuttack and Bhubaneswar. They are small leaders of this area who say something and do different. OK, if you all have the notice, then come with me to meet the Collector and tell him everything in detail. Your father has taken a LIC bond forty years back. You will show that to the Collector and tell him you belong to this country.

When he heard about the Collector, he was nervous. He dared not stand before the Collector; on the other hand, *Nimai Surgeon* shouted at him. He said- 'You have the LIC bond issued in India, which is forty years old. You can ask the Collector - Was the government sleeping for so many years?' If you can't stay in this country, ask him- 'Can you make us the citizens of *Bangladesh*?' If the Collector remains silent, say- 'We neither belong to this country nor that country, then shoot us.'

After listening to *Nimai Surgen* about Collector, he didn't have the courage. There is no use in pleading to anyone. To go to *Kendrapada* to meet the Collector by spending money means wasting one day's earnings. He was slightly stingy in this affair and didn't pay any attention to it. When he was returning, *Nimai* came with him to some distance. In the darkness, he kept his hand on his shoulder. He said- Dear *Bangladeshi*, sleep well with your family as you will go to *Chataka* in the morning again for fishing. Only seven days are left from the notice period, so come with me to *Kendrapada*.'

He told *Nimai Surgen* that he would go along with him and escape from there, but there were two things that *Nimai Surgen* said to him that lingered in his mind. He now knows that the *Utkal Bangiya Samiti* will never do anything for them and that only seven days are left to leave India.

He couldn't sleep properly at night. He had kept the door half closed, and the lamp was burning in the room. His pregnant wife was sleeping next to him. The notice had made him insane, and his wife looked like a black, dirty pig to him. He thought that she would give birth to a very different child. A child whose father would have been thrown out of the country before his birth. What will happen? Will his wife become a victim of the agents here? She will be sold somewhere.

At midnight, he sat on the bed and had vague thoughts about his wife. He thought of many fuzzy things like if a woman has a child, what is her value in the market?

Will any good person get married to his wife? Will she get a job for household work as she has a child? How do the labourers leave their children on the roadside and do their work? Can his wife, born and brought up in *Kolkata*, do this? His wife is young, and if she hadn't been pregnant, someone would have agreed to marry her after he left, or she could have worked as a servant in someone's house to make her living. After he goes, his wife will be in trouble because of the child. He felt the unborn child was an enemy for whom his wife would face problems in life. He lost the pride of being a father. There are only seven more days left. He felt he should speak to someone to make himself feel lighter. He woke his wife up from his sleep so that he could talk to her on this matter. His wife asked him-'What happened? What do you want to tell me at this point in time?'

-' Let's do one thing. You don't feel bad about it.'

-' No, no.' His wife smiled. He told her what was in his mind.

-' Let's go and abort this child.'

-' Have you become insane in the middle of the night? His wife shouted at him. He tried to make her understand and said-'After I leave, how will you live here alone with the child? If the child hadn't been there, you could have worked to earn your living, or someone would have agreed to marry you.'

His wife sobbed and said- I will sell fish, crab, and dry fish here and will take care of your child and live here. Please, don't kill my child.'

Whatever he thought just a while before became worthless in front of his wife's courage. He thought of his child as his enemy. He wiped the tears from his wife's eyes and kept his hand on her belly, whom he imagined as a pregnant pig a while ago. He caressed his wife. There were so many ways to come out of the nightmare. This was one of the ways.

It is his old routine to go to the bank of the river early in the morning and to check his *dinghy*. He did the same earlier in the morning. It was foggy and peaceful. Still, two of them were sitting on the bank of river *Gobari* and discussing the notice. He walked towards them and looked at their faces. They were *Mukul Rai and Nirmal Mondal,* who had also received the notice. Like him, the other people who received the notice also had sleepless nights. The only topic of discussion was the notice. He asked them-'What's new?'

Mukul Rai said- it's a severe matter. Many groups have come to *Jambu* to help those who received the notice.

He asked-'Who has come?'

-RSS people have come.

-'What is RSS?'

- 'They belong to *Rashtriya Swayamsevak Sangh*'

-' And what is that?'

Nirmal Rai got irritated and said- 'You must know Bharatiya Janata Party(BJP).' He nodded his head. *Nirmal Rai* said-' Along with the BJP is *RSS, Biswa Hindu Parisad and Bajrang Dal.* They have formed a *Sangha*, and this *Sangha* will help all the Hindus who have received the notice.'

Mukul Rai said-' In *Jambu* and *Ramnagar* area, Congress is against RSS. There was a fight between two young men in the *Jambu* market area yesterday. The young man who belongs to Congress said- 'You are all outsiders and follow communalism. Here, we will not appreciate any Sangha. This is our area. We will take care of the safety of these *Bangladeshi*s.'

The young man who belongs to RSS said,' We can't withdraw the notice by taking the donations from them, but our Sangha will show its power now.'

The man who belonged to Congress said-'We will safeguard our *Bangladeshi* brothers and sisters.'

The man who belonged to RSS said-'We will safeguard our *Bangladeshi* brothers and sisters.'

To safeguard was the issue and the reason for the fight between them. Now there is a tug of war between Congress and RSS.'

'What will happen now?'

'What will happen? Nothing….' *Nirmal Mondal* said.

Mukul Rai told him- 'Go and do your work. Whatever will happen, let it be. There was no fog when he returned, and the atmosphere was clear. From behind, he could hear *Nirmal Mondal* saying, ' Man.' Knowing *Nirmal* had a bad mouth, he didn't want to spoil his day by retaliating to what he said. In that way, *Mukul Rai* was a better person. A few good people like *Nimai Surgen* and *Mukul Rai* tried to explain and speak to him properly in this *Jalipada* area. He had come to check his *dinghy* and met these two people. He ignored what *Nirmal Mondal* said and looked at his *dinghy*. He felt his *dinghy* was looking at him in the soft sunlight. This *dinghy* is the only source of livelihood for him. He had varied thoughts about the *dinghy*. Will this *dinghy* be with me when I leave the country? He tried to make himself understand and sang a song- *'Hey! Dinghy, you have saved* us; we can earn a living because of you. Wherever I go, if there won't be a river like Gobari and a dinghy, then how will I live? My dinghy? He would have continued with his sad song, but his wife came and interrupted him and said-'Come and have tea.'

After three to four days, suddenly, the RSS people entered the village. All of them were wearing brown colour half pants and a white shirt, which was tugged in. The cap was pulled in their pocket. They went from one house to another and said -they would provide safety to you. Show us your papers. We will do the survey.' He spread a mat in the veranda of his house. Two of them sat on it, and by that time, there were already three to four of his refugee neighbours in his house, and among them was *Nimai Surgeon*. He wasn't ready to show his papers to the unknown people. Still, *Nimai Surgen* gave him an indication to deliver the documents so that something could be done.

He went inside the house to get the papers. His wife asked- who are they? Why will they see our papers? Will they throw you out from here? What will happen to me? How will I live with my baby alone in *Jambu*?'

He picked up the papers and told her-'Whatever you think it's not correct.' He took the documents from the old polythene bag and showed them individually. He showed them the LIC bond, the refugee certificate, voter ID, ration card, landed property documents, and all other documents he received from the government. He finally showed the notice he had received. One among them said he is a Hindu. Our Sangha will conduct a meeting here. It will be discussed in a meeting in *Ramnagar* and then in *Jambu*. In the forum, members of the *Sanga* family *Shri Ashok Sahu, Gyanendra Behera, Bikas Pal, Arjun Mondal, and Malati Hembrum* will join. You come to the meeting with a photocopy of your papers, and your name will be registered there. You have to sign or give your thumb impression in a form, and we won't take any money for this. We will take this matter to the High Court, so you should attend the meeting with your papers.'

He gave a slogan: 'Bharat Mata Ki Jai' and left. His wife was in the house listening to what they were saying. She again started crying as she always does. She said -they would get your thumb impression and frame you in a theft case. They will collect our papers and will take you somewhere. How will I survive here? How will my baby survive?' She continued crying. In between the chaos of the notice and RSS, his wife delivered the baby. There was no time to call the midwife. His wife, who had returned to her senses and was lying on the bed, couldn't speak properly and said in a feeble voice to him-'Make hot water and bring it quickly.'

He forgot all about the notice and started working as an experienced midwife. His wife had given birth to a lovely baby boy. He gave the baby to his wife, cut the umbilical cord to separate the baby from his mother, and cleaned the baby covered with blood with lukewarm water. The baby cried softly. Three ladies from their locality came to do what was needed. He came to know that he had nothing else to do there. The birth of the baby gave him momentary happiness. The thought of the notice and his child's future bothered him. He suddenly had a fever that took three to four days for him to recover. He took the malaria medicine painkiller and could recover. He learned there was a meeting after two days, and he had to submit copies of the papers.

The people who received the notice to submit the photocopy copy of their papers were in haste. Jambu had no photocopy machine, so the people were going either to *Ramnagar* or *Marshaghai. He* didn't have a bicycle for photocopying; on the other hand, his wife wanted to eat something good after the delivery. She was also ordering a few things for the baby. He thought half of the day would be wasted if he went to *Ramnagar* by walking for just a photocopy and returned. Still, as all of them were giving the photocopies of the papers, he had to provide the copies; otherwise, his name would not be deleted from the illegal migrant list.

He took the papers and went to *Nimai Surgen* and said-' I can't rely upon anyone and give the documents to photocopy because if the pieces get lost, then I will lose all the evidence certificates. So, please take fifty rupees, go in your motorcycle, and get the photocopy done.' *Nimai Surgen* gave him back fifty rupees and said-' I am going to *Marsaghai* for my business purpose, so I will get the photocopy done. They will take only four to five rupees for the photocopy, so don't worry. He gave *Nimai Surgen* all the papers and went back home. As soon as he entered the house, he could hear the baby crying, which brought an unknown fear in him. He became emotional with that fear and thought- I don't have any identity proof with me at present, and if the police come and ask me to go away, what would I do? He started crying louder than the baby. Both father and son were crying. His wife took the child and fed him, then wiped his tears and said, ' You are now the father of a child. Why are you crying like a child?' She comforted him, and he cooled down.

All of them got ready and went together for the meeting. The people who received the notice had photocopies of the papers. They discussed that they had already paid money to *Utkal Bangiya Samiti*, but they didn't do anything. These people won't take money from us and will fight for us in court by spending on their own. Suppose we can again become Indians without paying anything. Why shouldn't we accept whatever will be decided in the meeting? Another person who had all the news about politics said- 'They aren't like *Surakshya Samiti*; it is an All India party. They have demolished Babri Masjid, and many great politicians like *Atal Bihari Bajpayee* are associated with them. They perform *Ratha Yatra* to get votes from Hindus, and as we are Hindus, they have come to protect us. Their motive is to keep us in India.'

He was listening to them and was moving ahead with a firm belief that he would stay in India. The place was crowded, and a camp was set up. He entered his name in a list in the camp and gave the photocopy papers thumb impression in a form for court proceedings. He could only hear about Hindus in the meeting. One of the speakers who spoke about the *Bangladesh War* said- 'before the *Bangladesh*, the Hindus were in trouble. They killed the Hindu children by hitting them on the wall, raped and tortured the Hindu ladies and girls, hacked their breast, and sent it to India by train. They have done many heinous crimes. They have converted many Hindus to Muslims forcibly. The family of the *Bangladesh* President Abdul Mohammad Biswas was Hindu. Does any Muslim have *'Biswas'* as a surname?

Other examples are *Bangladesh's Ghani Khan Choudhary and Golam Ali Mondal*. These were all Hindus. To disgrace Hindus, all converted Muslims inserted names like Abdul Khan, Mohammad, etc., before their surname as they didn't want to leave their wealth and property there. They inserted Sheikh, Ali, and Khan names, grew their beard and moustache, and read *Namaz*. Though they were Hindus by birth, they dressed up like Muslims, but those who left *Bangladesh* and came to India as refugees were all Hindus. They have come to this country to save their religion. Once upon a time, India was one, but because of the conspiracy, India is now divided into three pieces. Remember that it doesn't matter where the Hindus stay in India. They belong to India. My dear Hindu brothers and sisters, we have come, so there is nothing to worry about. Bharat Mata Ki Jai.'

All of them shouted the same slogan. Though sitting at the back of the meeting, he still raised his hand and gave the slogan. After listening to the speech about Hindus, he was excited. Another Hindu leader stood up and encouraged the *Bangladeshi*s and said-' You have received the voter ID card of this country, and if you are all illegal migrants, then why is the voter ID given to you? This notice is a foul play of politics with a hidden motive; otherwise, the right people would have received the message. At *Kharnasi*, two Hindu people have received the notice, which proves that the notice is based on incorrect information. We will challenge this notice in court. We will file a case in court for those who have given us a photocopy of their papers. When the date is fixed in the court, those people will come to the court with their original documents and provide the evidence. That's all. Remember one thing- You are all Hindus and belong to Hindustan, so pursue your livelihood as you did by catching fish and crabs from river *Gobari*. *Jai Hind*.'

All of them gave the slogan- *Jai Hind* and dispersed. After he crossed *Jambu ghat*, he heard a loud voice of a Congressman. He said-' Are you supporting BJP after *Ramnagar* meeting? You all *Bangladeshi*s, how can you forget Indira Gandhi?'

All of them heard it but pretended as if they didn't listen to it. They quickly walked away from there as they knew that these small leaders in the village thought about their own benefit but not about the party. If they answer back to them, then they will use foul language. A person with them heard the Congressman abusing them and said-' Yes, the time has changed. Indira Gandhi brought us here and settled us down, but that was long back. After Indira Gandhi, were there any leaders like her in the Congress Party? You are now speaking about Congress, and during the *Surakshya Committee* meeting, Congress leaders were also present. You have taken money from us to help us regarding the notice but didn't do anything. Instead, you divided the collected bounty among yourselves and dissolved the *Samiti*. How can you speak like that?' The people who got the notice are bold now as they heard that there would be a case in the High Court through *Viswa Hindu Parishad*. He heard that *Pravash Mondal*, who works in *Paradeep*, also has received the notice, and he has filed a case in the High Court and is spending a lot of money. He felt as if the whole world was fighting against this notice.

In between, a month given to leave the country was over. Those who stopped doing their regular work again started working. They started repairing the net, the engine, and the boat and waited for a full moon day. He also realized that if he didn't go to *Chataka*, it would be challenging to manage the house.

Whenever he had time to sit quietly while fishing, many stray thoughts ran through his mind and troubled him. He felt like he was just a piece of paper in which the notice was typed in English and served inside a brown envelope. Not only he but all the fishermen who were fishing there and have received the notice are like the prisoners of that brown envelope in which the notice was served by the government- as if these people will fall into the water and dissolve like a piece of paper.

Gossip regarding the notice was in the air for months together. *Nimai Surgen* said that after a month if no steps are taken by the government as a solution, they may be sitting quietly. Government processes take a lot of time. Another notice may come when it is mentioned to leave the country within a week. There is politics in everything.'

He often gets up from a deep sleep at midnight and recollects those scary dreams. He dreamt that he had received a government notice to leave within a week, and after a week, two policemen standing in front of his house saying- 'Leave this country immediately'. He would leave the house, keeping behind his wife, crying, his son crawling towards him, and those two policemen dragging him away. They would be dropping him in a country, but he couldn't remember which country it was.

He imagined himself in the *Chataka* for fishing in his small *dinghy*. He could see a tourist boat speeding towards him, and the man in the boat would shout, 'The police are searching for you.' Suddenly, his hands became cold just thinking about the nightmare.

He returned to his village and heard people saying that there was a mention in the newspaper- 'These illegal migrants of *Bangladesh* are spies in this country; they are also trafficking *ayurvedic* medicines; mixing beef with goat meat and selling; printing fake notes; selling kerosene in black, and acting as pimps. They have forcibly occupied *Jambu* and have made it a mini *Bangladesh*.'

The charges which were brought against *Bangladeshis* in *Jambu* were mean and ugly. Whatever incidents happened during that time, the illegal migrants were held responsible. He was staying at home and playing with his son, trying to fulfil his wife's small wishes, and going to *Chataka* to earn his living, but there was always a fear within him. One day *Nimai Surgen* called him and said-,' I came to know that you are sometimes not going to *Chataka* and sitting at home and crying. Try to understand that in this country, many wrong notices are framed; again, those weren't worked upon. It's a part of the political game. The RSS people filled out a petition, and a date was given by the court, but none of you went to the court to give evidence in fear, and because of that, your case couldn't be considered. The case against the notice is still in the court, so now you are all swinging between *Bangladesh* and India. You will be here in India till your death and won't be sent away. Now you have to look after your child and family. You are swinging between India and *Bangladesh*, but did you think about your son?'

He gave a blank look to *Nimai Surgen*. *Nimai* said- they were born in *Kolkata*, stayed in *Jambu*, and are *Bangladeshi* illegal migrants. Your son is born in *Jambu*, and if a notice comes in his name, will he be called an Indian? He will also become a *Bangladeshi*. Do you want him to stay in fear in this country for life? I don't think you want that way.'

After listening to *Nimai Surgen*, he was taken aback. What will happen to his son? He couldn't find a way out, and at that time, *Nimai Surgen* said-' The son of a *Bangladeshi* father can be Indian, and for that, a birth certificate is required.' He thought it was impossible as all the dealers and offices had their names listed as illegal migrants. Who will give a birth certificate to his son?

Nimai Surgen gave him an example and said-' In *Jambu, Sujit Mondal* has received the notice. Then why have government officials issued his son a birth certificate? The child of an illegal migrant born here is Indian.' *Nimai Sugen* kept his hand on his back and said, ' You fool! These things take time to be done here. The government officials need two thousand rupees as a bribe for this.'

He lost his senses when he heard about bribing. He didn't know how to bribe and also didn't know how the person takes bribes. He thought about it and became silent. *Nimai* explained - you would give the mediator two thousand rupees. He will do the rest of the work and give you the paper. The illegal migrant issue is a vicious circle. You may hang between the uncertainties till your death, but remember that if you get the birth certificate, then it will be helpful for your son in the future.'

By giving a bribe of two thousand rupees to the government official, our son can become an Indian. He told this to his wife. His wife, who understands only half of the things, was afraid and said-' No, no, we won't give the bribe. If the government officials come, then I will tell them- 'I am Indian., I don't have a notice in my name, and as I have given birth, he belongs to this country.' He was annoyed with his wife and said-' What do you know? No one will believe what you say, and all of them will look for the papers.'

His wife finally understood what a better and safer

future meant for their son, but still, she said-' From where will we get two thousand rupees?' He spoke bravely to his wife-' To give a bribe to be an Indian in this country, fishing is the only way to earn.' He said this and left the house.

He went towards the *Chataka* in his *dinghy*.

CHAPTER -5

Despite all these incidents, there were many dinghies in the estuary of river Kapali. On one side of the Chataka was Balikuda; on the other side lay bare the Bay of Bengal and the islands. There was a green island, a port at the False Point -Hukitola.

He could hear strange sounds from the port at *False Point (False Point is a low headland in the Bay of Bengal. It is located in the Kendrapada district of Odisha, India. The point derives its name from the circumstance that vessels proceeding up the Bay of Bengal frequently mistook it for Point Palmyra, less than a degree farther north.).* He got up from the bed in fear, sat on his bed, and looked around the room. He was seventy-two years old at that time. What happens to a person who gets up at midnight at this age? He goes to the washroom, drinks water, and doesn't fall asleep afterwards. There was still a long time for the sunrise. He looked around the room, and finally, his eyes got stuck on the old door made during British rule.

He felt as if he was a ghost. He was scared and peed on his clothes. He thought- Now it's time for his death. He is going to die soon. The *Chataka* is far in the estuary of river *Gobari*; on the other side of the *Chataka* is the port of *False Point*, and from there, how can he hear the strange sounds in his old age when he can't hear properly?

Once upon a time, his father also heard these strange sounds at midnight, and his father stammered and said- 'Hu- Ki- Tola.' Then he died, pointing towards the door. He also heard the call. Will he die? Why does this strange sound of the port at the *False Point* take away the life of his family member? He was trying to survive on this strange, scary night as he still dared to live for more years.

He immediately turned away his eyes from the door towards the black and white picture hung on the colourless wall, concentrating on that picture frame. It was the photograph of his father, taken in the port itself. His father was there in the uniform, standing solid and stout. He diverted his attention from the door and the strange sound and thought about his father and his childhood days. If he can still think about his childhood days, how can he ever die then?

father always told stories whenever he returned from the port to home. Those stories were about the port. In the year 1877, there was a drought in *Odisha*. At that time, the *Britishers* at *Cuttack* announced that there would be a series of droughts in *Odisha*, so a port should be constructed for importing rice from outside.

After getting the announcement, *Mr. Ravenshaw* was excited. He called the Collector *Macpherson* to his house and asked- 'Who are the British officers here who can give an idea to construct a port?' *Macpherson* told the name- '*J.H. Walker*. He is known as *Mr Huki Walker* here. He was the Superintend Engineer in the Irrigation Department.'

To find a place for the port, *Ravenshaw*, along with *Macpherson* and *Walker*, went in a steamer through the *Mahanadi* estuary. At a little distance from the estuary, in the middle of the sea, *Walker* pointed to an island and said-' This is the *False Point*. Previously, at this place, the boats crashed. That's why near to it is a lighthouse.'

At the place where *Mahanadi* and the river *Gobari* meet the sea, there is a lake that is two to three kilometres long called *Chataka*. On the other side of *Chataka* is a mangrove forest island. He pointed at that deserted island and said-' Big boats can put their anchor there. This island is at a small distance from the bank of the river. Already *Cuttack-Marshaghai* canal work is over, so through the waterway, required things can be transported to Cuttack.'

Huki *Walker* had an idea about *Jambu*knot, river *Gobari*, *Chataka*, *Batighara*, and *False Point*. He was hard working and also knew the techniques to make others work. He was a very clever engineer. *Ravenshaw* thought building the port as soon as possible would be better. If rice can be imported from Rangoon, then it will be helpful for people during the famine; otherwise, the government will be seen in a poor light.

acpherson looked at the *False Point* of the island and said-' We have to build two sheds here. One is for the boats and the other to keep the grains.' *Ravenshaw* immediately agreed to it and said,' If this is the right place to build a port, then I will recommend it fast so that funds can be released immediately.'

Three of them were very happy with the outcome of the visit and wanted to organize a party. They stayed in the bungalow at *Batighara* and had champagne. An idea struck *Ravenshaw*, and he asked- 'What will we name this island? Accordingly, we will maintain the records for the port construction.'

By then, oldie *Huki Walker* had drunk two pegs of champagne. Drunkenly, he lit his cigar and babbled about *Armstrong and Eliot*. He was also reminiscent of the place Windy Elias, where he was born. *Ravenshaw* realized they needed to give a suitable name for the port they discussed. *Macpherson* could also recognise the need to name the place and suggested, ' Can we call the site *Hukitola* as per the name of *Mr Huki Walker*?' After listening to Macpherson's suggestion, *Huki Walker* was pleased that a port would be named after him. *Macpherson* tried to make *Ravenshaw* understand and said-' The word '*Huki*' means '*Termitary*' and '*Tola*' means ' *Hata*' in the local language. So, the people of *Odisha* will readily accept the name '*Hukitola*'.'

Ravenshaw was already drunk. He said-' Nice name'. *Hukitola*'.' In that champagne party, the name *Hukitola* was finally approved.

His father was working as a dockyard worker in the *Hukitola* port. He wasn't only a dockyard worker but did many other harbour assignments. Sometimes, he worked with the carpenters and additional time in the office. People working in all the departments in the port liked him for his workmanship. He worked really hard for everyone's satisfaction in the harbour area.

After two to three months, when his father returned home on leave, he brought many goodies for them- foreign chocolates, the old clothes of the officials, Burma lanterns, and many more items. People of the village came to their houses to look at these items. During his visit to the village, his father was away from home. He went to *Jambu's* marketplace, *Ramnagar*, to meet his friends and sometimes to *Baulagadi*. Whenever he was at home, he drank foreign liquor and said-' I am not drinking too much liquor these days. In the *Hukitola* port, the highest official, Captain Harris, is the biggest drunkard in the world. That person has put his heart and soul into building *Hukitola*.'

Sometimes, his father talks about Harris. He says-'One of my friends helped me to meet that English official. It was evening, and Harris was sitting on the deck of the *'Ghajipur'* boat, which had anchored there. He was sitting in the dim light with a glass and a water bottle on the table. Under the table was a small hip flask. He poured the glass with liquor every fifteen to twenty minutes, added water, drank, and smoked. The friend pointed towards the man and said-'He is Captain Harris.'

Hukitola port was surrounded by a marshy forest. Captain Harris hoisted a flag so that from a distance, the boats and steamers approaching *Hukitola* could see it with their binoculars and make out about the port's existence. Through the *Marsaghai* canal, Captain Harris brought the stones from Cuttack to construct a building and a couple of small huts for offices, port workers, and sailors. With Harris's weekly efforts, the cargo boat *'Ghajipur'* anchored here. Though it wasn't too big, it wasn't too small either. There was a basement to keep the goods; there were many rooms- a kitchen, a washroom, and a broad deck. It also had many other facilities. *'Ghajipur '*looked like a floating hotel. The British officials who came from Cuttack through the canal reached here and boarded *'Ghajipur'* to go to *Kolkata*. Whenever ' *Ghajipur'* was anchored, the place would be crowded with British people, and they had fun and frolic.

Once in a month or two, a couple of boats from France anchored in *Hukitola*. Quite often, cargo boats from Rangoon and Mauritius came here and anchored. 'The port will be more active as more vessels will come from different places'- Harris wrote letters to various port offices.

The old man sailor 'Black' was always there along with the stern and rigid working officer Harris. This old sailor was very knowledgeable and artistic. He brought the goldsmiths from Cuttack and made them do silver filigree work on the guest house doors and office. Harris and Black always worked hard to make *Hukitola* Port more beautiful. After the end of the famine, *Ravenshaw* became a little stingy and needed to approve more money for the development of *Hukitola* Port. Because of such misery, they both were unhappy as they planned to make the port look more beautiful.

During the cyclone, an old cargo boat which needed repair and maintenance reached there from *Kolkata*. Black, who had an artistic mind, looked at the valuable wood and iron used in the old boat. One day, when he was sitting and drinking with Harris, he said-' You must know that a big, partially destroyed cargo boat has come to our port.' Suddenly, the design of one of the offices in Britain stuck with him. He said-' If we can break the boat and use the wood to make the floor and walls of your office, then your office will look nothing less than the offices in Britain.' Harris nodded in support of his proposal. But with apprehension, he said -' If *Kolkata* port enquires? What will happen if we get the government's notice to auction the old boat and deposit the money?'

-' You can write that the boat hit the *False Point* and was destroyed. We can't trace the remaining parts of the boat as it got drowned.'

Harris and Black dreamt that *Hukitola* Port's office should look beautiful like the offices in London. Invariably, a lie is hidden within beauty. He poured the rest of the liquor into his glass and lighted a cigar. Harris drafted a rough letter to the *Kolkata* port office sitting on the boat's *Ghajipur* deck. He wrote – 'One of your boats hit *Hukitola False Point* during the cyclone and was destroyed. It has submerged in the sea. We tried to find the submerged boat, but it's untraceable.' In that letter, he included one more request to give one boat with an engine and a cargo boat as *Hukitola* port is expanding.

It doesn't matter how much Harris drinks or speaks, but he always considered improving the *Hukitola* Port. Harris learned there was a shortage of drinking water in *Hukitola* as they got saline water wherever it was dug to get drinking water. He took the advice of the engineers and the irrigation department. He made the arrangements so that the rainwater from the roof of the buildings would flow down to four big water potholes. He also made an underground rainwater harvesting system, and the water was filtered with bleaching to make it appropriate for drinking. In this way, drinking water was available throughout the year in *Hukitola*.

His father never forgets to narrate stories about *Hukitola* and Harris. But one day, his father returned to *Jambu*. He was sobbing. The neighbours came and surrounded him. His father beat his chest and said-' Harris Saheb! Hey! Captain Harris. You are no more. What will happen to this *Hukitola* port? Captain, you took the boat in the Suez Canal and have undergone a voyage in the Indian Ocean. Why did you stop near *Hukitola* port? Why did you render your service for the development of the port? You were disgraced because of that. You tried your best so the port works appropriately, and finally, you got drowned in this port itself and died.'

His father couldn't control his emotions. He went near his father and tried to console him. He said- 'If Harris Sahib drowned and died, then the British government will send somebody else to *Hukitola*.'

' But who can be like Captain Harris?' His father said. The next day, his father controlled his emotion and said-' I will go to *Hukitola* today. Harris Sahib isn't there. Now, the amount of work in the port has increased. If we all do our job well, then *Hukitola* Port will prosper.'

Father had a lot of responsibility in the port. He was accustomed to the surroundings of the port and the people over there. How can he sit at home without any work? He was restless and went to *Hukitola*. He worked there for four to five months, didn't come home even once, and after multiple messages from us, he finally returned. On his return, he wasn't jovial; he had grown his beard, and his hair was without oil. After Captain Harris drowned and died, *Hukitola* Port encountered many troubles, and the bad days started for my father. There was a story from Kolkata that spoke about *Hukitola*'s future. This railway line will run from Kolkata to Madras. The survey was over, and there was good progress on laying the railway tracks.

The government and contractors are working on it. Grand Trunk road work from Madras to *Kolkata* will also begin. After the railroad and roads become operational, will the cargo boats come to *Hukitola* and anchor there? The cargo train has started running from *Kolkata*, and the passenger train will start soon. Will the floating city *'Ghajipur'* anchor in future at *Hukitola* to take the British travellers to *Kolkata*? Everyone will prefer to go by train as the time will be less. Why will they board the boat and steamer? If the steamer doesn't sail, then the port will be closed.

Whatever he foretold gradually became a reality. It was time for his father to return home. A crowded port like *Hukitol* was slowly being deserted. Boats no more came and anchored there. The Port Authority of France wrote a letter to the *Kolkata* Port Authority.

It informed that *Hukitola* port was becoming shallow because of the Mahanadi delta. Hence, the boats from France were not able to anchor there. There were no more officers like Captain Harris to bring the equipment to *Hukitola* to build the port infrastructure. Cuttack's Commissioner's office needed to provide more revenue to improve *Hukitola* Port. The *Bengali* officers advised the *Kolkata* Port Authority to close *Hukitola* Port. The cargo boats from Rangoon started loading and unloading the cargo in *Kolkata* port instead of *Hukitola*. The officers posted in *Hukitola* were ordered to vacate and transferred to other ports. As the port was no longer in use, the infrastructure was ruined. The buildings were in an awry condition. The port, built faster to manage the famine, withered quickly and closed in 1924.

The British officials posted there disappeared in steamers; the Indian port workers and labourers lost their jobs and returned home. Along with them, emotionally shattered, his father returned to *Jambu*.

No more stories about Hukitola could be heard from his father. It was difficult for him to arrange money daily for liquor, so he settled with opium. He purchased poppy seeds, crushed them, boiled them in water, and drank four to five times daily, without which his body would shiver. He had no work and was always intoxicated.

At that time, there was a rumour in *Jambu* that people were stealing things from *Hukitola*. Captain Harris and Black brought the goldsmith from Cuttack and got the silver filigree work done on the doors, and now those are stolen. All the precious things in the port were stolen. The *Bangladeshi, Kanthi, Vardhaman, and Maedinpur* fishermen who go fishing to *Chataka* have stolen the stuff from *Hukitola*.

Then, he was a young boy. He had the strength to cross river *Gobari* by rowing the boat alone. After his father stopped working, he flew to *Chataka* to fish. During that time, he became friendly with a *Bangladeshi* named *Sadhan Mondal*.

Between 1958 and 1964, many *Bangladeshi*s came to *Jambu, Mahakalpada, Marshaghai,* and *Kendrapada*. Others went to different places in *Odisha*, which had rivers like *Bangladesh*. They cleared the marshy forest land and took up fishing as an occupational source for their living. Only a few were farming in *Bangladesh*, and others had businesses. After reaching there, all of them turned into skilled fishermen.

One day, when all the fishermen were busy at *Chataka* in their *dinghy* for fishing, *Sadhan Mondal* pointed at *Hukitola*. He said, ' We both will go there in the night. If anything is left, there…. *Sadhan Mondal* was planning to steal. He mockingly told *Sadhan Modal*, 'Are all *Bangladeshi*s thieves like you?

-'What about the people from *Maedinpur*? Are you all saints? You people came to *Jambu*, cleaned the marshy forest, occupied *Jambu* for farming, built ponds, and did fishing in *Chataka*. We left our country and came here because we were scared and wanted to save our lives. We also followed the same path as we could to earn our living. *Sadhan Mondal* tried to make him comprehend and said-' Did you know *Dada*? In this world, everyone resorts to unfair means because of hunger. If the craving is satisfied, they all turn into saints.'

Sadhan Mondal gave a lot of arguments to rationalize stealing by citing many examples. He also thought that his father had spent his life in that port. Everything in *Hukitola* is a part of the blood and sweat of his father.

The night turned into an intense dark umbrella as he propelled the boat. It was almost midnight in *Chataka*. On that eventful moonlit night, he and *Sadhan Mondal* reached *Hukitola* and anchored the boat without anybody's knowledge. With the help of a small torch light that *Sadhan Mondal* owned, they started searching for some valuables to take back home.

In the beginning, they were scared of that deserted port. The place was surrounded by dense bushes and taller, old trees. The abandoned building was dark inside. Both of them could enter the hall with the help of the torchlight. There was nothing in that hall. Everything was already ransacked. People have already taken away the doors, windows, and even the iron grill which was attached to the window.

They went near the pole in the port to find out if they could find handmade old iron lumber anywhere. They can sell the old rusted iron to the vendor and earn some money if they find the old rusted iron. They couldn't find anything there also. There were only a few wooden doors that were lying on the floor. They could discover that the thieves had taken so many valuable things from there that they left the wooden doors just like that.

Sadhan Mondal asked-' What will we do?'

-' What else can we do? What is left here that we can steal? *Sadhan Mondal* ignored what he said, laughed, and said, ' We are not professional thieves. How can we return from here empty-handed? We could get one-half of the door. We will take that and divide it into two halves.'

There is a need to have some time or a place to divide the bounty. He felt as if the ghost in the deserted place was after them. He could hear the footsteps in the corridor, the typewriter from a room, and he could feel someone's breath near his ears. He could listen to the people's murmuring when they got down from the boat, the engine of the steamer switching off, and the tired voices of the port workers. He could feel the footsteps of his hardworking father, who worked there. He was surrounded by many puzzles and mysteries. After some time, he carried that door and walked towards his boat.

He said-' Listen, *Sadhan*! My father worked here as a dockyard worker. The port was closed. My father is now old and addicted to drugs and nearing death. If I fix this door in my house, my father will look at it and remember his days in *Hukitola*, and maybe he will be better health-wise and live for a few more days. I will take this piece of the door for my father.'

After listening to him, *Sadhan Modal* was silent. When they got off the boat, he asked-' What did I get?' He sat on that door in resentment and said-' I will give you some money for your expenditure. This door isn't a big thing.'

One day, he took out the door made with mango wood and fixed it in the house. He set the door from *Hukitola* on the courtyard. It was inconvenient for everyone to cross the door as it was narrow, but they liked the door due to the intricate designs engraved on it. His father could make out and asked-' Tell me the truth, whose entrance is this?'

-' I have bought it. It was there in someone's house in *Marsaghai*.'

- Tell me the truth. Who had this door in *Marsaghai, Mahakalpada, Baulakani* or *Ramnagar*? I think I have seen this door somewhere.'

He thought it was better to tell the truth to the old man. He said-' After the port was closed, people took away everything from *Hukitola*. As you worked hard in *Hukitola*, you have a share of it. I could get only one piece of this door. Let your port's entrance be in front of you.'

' Rascal! Where did I earn my living from there? You brought this door and said the *Hukitola* would be before my eyes? I want something other than *Hukitola*. The day Captain Harris got drowned, *Hukitola* Port also got drowned. Take away this door.'

For the first time, he gathered enough courage to bring happiness to his father. He resorted to thievery, but his father was not willing to accept that door. His father was getting irritated because of his age and his adamant behaviour. As he grew older and looked at the door, he became increasingly resistant. He screamed-'Throw away this. Take it away from here.'

-' Yes, I will remove the door after a few days.

-' Yes, break the door into pieces and use it for firewood.'

-' Yes, I will do that, but there is a shortage of money to purchase a new door, so I will do it after a few days.'

He prolonged the matter on removing the door, and suddenly, one night, the old man woke up from his sleep and said-' I can hear the scary sounds from *Hukitola*. I am going to die.' In the morning, he passed away. When his father was around, he was carefree. But now, he had the burden of the family.

After quite a few days, there was a discussion on *Hukitola* again. Sitting near the tea stall, the fishermen from *Chataka* in *Jambu* were discussing- Now *Hukitola* will again be revived as the government has started the survey work.

In 1967, *Singh Deo* became the Chief Minister as an Independent candidate. *Rajendra Narayan Singh Deo* was the son of Patna King *Prithvi Raj Singh Deo*. He toured worldwide and wanted to do something for the development of *Odisha*, like his royal family. He formed his ministry with an independent party, the *Utkal Congress*, and took a few independent MLAs with him. *Singh Deo* called all the ministers for a meeting. Said your respective departments, wherever any work is incomplete, you can carry out the unfinished work.'

Mr Murali Prasad Mishra was the Cabinet Minister of the Forest Department, and *Mr Brindaban Mishra* was his deputy. *Brindaban Mishra* had an idea about the project. The Deputy Minister proposed the same to the Cabinet Minister and said-' In our *Athagarh* forest division under *Kujanga*

Yojana is *Jambu* and *Mahakalpada* area. During the British rule, there was a port in *False Point- Hukitola*. It is necessary to open a bit of house for our forest department there because the *Bangladeshi*s staying in that area are stealing. There is no substantial investment in building a bit house. An old building in the port can be repaired; doors and windows can be fixed. We can appoint a Forest officer, a Pontoon boat driver, and three to four forest guards.'

Murali Prasad Mishra knew there would be an election in 1971. It was the order of *Singh Deo* to carry out the necessary work in their ministry, so after listening to the plan of Deputy Minister *Brindaban Mishra*, he said-' I will speak to the Chief Minister regarding this proposal, and then we will contact *Athgarh* division. All the work should be done slowly but perfectly.'

Government procedure takes a lot of time. It took almost three years to begin the work. In 1970, the old port's repair work started. Many forest officers travelled by the Pontoon boat to supervise the work. But when the work started, many forest department workers requested that the forest officers avoid sending them to *Hukitola*.

The forest officer appointed from the *Kujanga* zone in *Hukitola* didn't stay there. Sometimes, he would visit *Hukitola* and return to stay with his family in *Jagatsinghpur*. The forest guards who were on duty in *Hukitola* took leave and stayed back at home. There was a discussion among the forest workers regarding the ghosts in *Hukitola*. The Ranger thought if the Bit house was there and the workers didn't stay, he would lose his job or be transferred anytime. He felt that as he was not staying there often going back to his family in the capital, he couldn't say anything to the forest officers at *Jagatsinghpur*. So he had an idea. He firmly told one of the forest guards- *'Natabar Pradhan,* as you are appointed for this job, you must stay in *Hukitola's* Bit house.'

There was no other option for *Natabar,* so he took his belongings and went to *Hukitola.* There was no work over there. He spent his time sitting in the Bit house and listening to the sound of the sea. He cooked his own food before the sunset, ate, and slept. The ministers were sleeping peacefully in their houses, and the thieves were cutting down the trees from the forest without fear.

There was a cyclone in the coastal area in 1971. Rain began at midnight and turned into a hurricane. The storm submerged *Jambu* and *Mahkalpada.* The hurricane destroyed everything. Dead bodies and animal carcasses were seen floating in the river *Gobari.* Altogether, 1336 people died in the *Jambu* area. After the storm passed, people again started constructing their broken houses. They repaired the boats and nets and were again ready to go fishing. People also demanded compensation for the destruction. Suddenly, there was news that the forest guard *Natabara Pradhan's* dead body was hanging on a tree.

Many people died in the 1971 cyclone, but his family was safe. The day he heard that *Natabar Pradhan* was dead during the hurricane, he was shocked. Intoxicated, his father used to say, ' Captain Harris is there in *Hukitola.* No one can survive there.'

Over some time, he wanted to forget about *Hukitola.* Still, the single door in his house always reminded him of the place. He remembered the night he went to *Hukitola* to steal and his father's death. He told his son-' Remove this door from here and fix another door.'

His son was also busy with his business and involved in politics. He was in the *Utkal Congress Party.* They planned to remove *Rajendra Narayan Singh Deo* from the chief minister position and make *Biswanath Das* the next chief minister. He was spending money from his pocket and trying to motivate people against Singh Deo. He didn't heed what his father said and was annoyed when he was told to remove it.

He said, ' If I remove the door from here and fix another door, all the neighbours will mock me. They will say that we sold the stolen door to someone else again. You have brought the door and have fixed it here. It's not a door –it's a soar. Why will you fiddle with it now? Let it be there.'

He couldn't say anything after listening to his son. He recalled he also didn't heed what his father told him sometime back, and now his son is doing the same. How many sons in the world really do listen to their father? His eyes were filled with tears. He has stolen once in his life, which pinched him lifelong.

The strange sounds of *Hukitola*'s dead port will never end as long as the door is in his house. Like his father, the sounds will continue to hunt him till his death. He tried to divert his attention from the strange sounds, but like his father's case, they would return in the dead of the night. He will be thinking about his father and the strange sounds at night, and the days rolled over the nights to bring back those old memories. He would feel like living in *Jambu* for a few more days and ignoring the sound. The early morning wind blowing from the riverside will make him muster the courage to live for a day. In the morning, the family will serve him *halwa* made from wheat, black tea and a glass of water. He couldn't chew things after losing all his teeth.

One day in the morning, he didn't eat or drink anything; he took a pinch of tobacco and stood up to remove that mysterious door as he couldn't walk through the door with a stick; he had enough courage to wipe out his sins of the past and remorse of not listening to the father. Will he be able to do so on that very day?

CHAPTER -6

The port was destroyed. The old forest vanishes through the footpaths of life from the refugee colonies. The old breeze and old water flow just like that. Despite being the oldest, the lighthouse stood upright like an ever-vigil onlooker. - The Lighthouse (Batighara).

There was still time for the sunset. He stood atop the hundred and forty feet high balcony. From the bottom, it looks like an infant of a black monkey.

His father was also like him. Right from his youth to his old age, he climbed the staircase of the lighthouse and stood on the balcony. He couldn't stand straight in his old age. His father, standing on the top terrace, looked like a foal.

Once, his father stumbled on the staircase of the lighthouse, broke his hip, and was bedridden for four months. After the recovery, being occasionally breathless, he again climbed up the stairs of the lighthouse. His father now sat at home with a bent spine like a bow. His stepmother spoke to the light-keeper and engaged him instead of his father.

Sometimes, standing alone on the lighthouse balcony, he thinks- there is no difference between him and his father. They are the same and continue in the same job of cleaning the lantern.

His last duty starts with the passage of the day. He tells the visitors of the lantern room around the circular balcony to get down the staircase - 'Leave now. Go downstairs. It's already time.' He enters the lantern room, stands on a table, and removes the log white curtains around the glasses. He wipes the lantern and the prism and sweeps the room. After completing the day's work, he locks the lantern room, stands on the balcony and looks down –the light keeper would be looking at his watch.

All the *batti (a loosely woven cord (in a candle or oil lamp) that draws fuel by capillary action up into the flame or any piece of twine that conveys liquid by capillary action) are* not lit together in one go. It depends on the time of sunset. For the months when the sun sets in at 5.48 pm, the lighthouse is lighted at 5.45 pm. There is a timetable here regarding the sunrise and sunset. In October, the light will be lit at 5.15 pm; in March, the lights will be switched off at 6.10 am.

The light-keeper looks at the watch and switches on the light accordingly. Then, one can see the light beams from the lighthouse in the Bay of Bengal, River *Kharnasi*, *Jambu*, *Mahakalpada*, and *Hukitola*.

Once the lights are on, it means the end of your duty. He climbs down the sixteen iron stairs, hundred and forty-eight concrete stairs, and finally reaches the lighthouse door, then locks it. In front of the switch room, under a casuarina tree, on a concrete bench, in the shadows of light and darkness, in this twenty-six-acre land, like arguing ghosts, the light-keeper and two signal men sit to break the desolation by their discussions. He hands over the keys to the light keeper and returns home.

Light-keeper stops him. He runs towards the grocery store to replenish his depleting consumables; he fills buckets of water from the noisy tube- -well in his quarter into his tank, warms his left out food of the afternoon; works as a servant for the family-less housekeeper's quarter as a maidservant of British era. He assumes this to be part of his duty.

He switches the torchlight and starts towards the dark colony. Along the compound wall of the lighthouse, beneath the old mango trees, around that dense and dark area, lies the graveyard of white people. There are skeletons of white fellas in those cemeteries. Thinking on this matter, he feels a bit frightened. His throat becomes dry. He feels as if the eyes of those ten marble tombs are staring at him. In that pitch darkness, without any fuss, he advances carefully.

After his father's death, he started working regularly in the lighthouse. While finishing the menial work in the light keeper's house and returning back home, he was always frightened near this place. He was returning to his colony after the light keeper guided him by showing the torchlight and helping him cross the graveyard. Once a night, to remove his fear, the light-keeper held a torch in one hand and pulled him into the cemetery with the other hand. He had made ten white fellas stand before him by focusing the torch on the marble pieces on the tombs. He sat near the graves and roamed around to touch them. He also let him feel the tombs and caressing one of the tombs, he said- 'He is Smith. He came here in 1843 on December 12th, and this is the tomb of Smith's 24-year-old daughter Merlin. Both father and daughter are here. He is Captain Harris. Captain

Harris and Captain Black did a lot to improve *Hukitola* Port. Harris got drowned and died in *Hukitola*. In 1877, his friend Black made a beautiful tomb for him.'

Look at these little kids. They were born in *Batighara* but couldn't grow up. She is Anne. This little cutie pie was only one year and two months old. He is Edward- He was only one year and one month old. She is- Daisy Grary- She was five years, seven months, and eleven days old. Once upon a time, she played around in the lighthouse colony, and now she is here. Look at the tomb of Grary. They have engraved beautiful lines on the marble-

'*The sparrow died*

Death came like a friend

The bud which was supposed to bloom on the earth

Finally Bloomed in heaven.'

And this ill-fated Stewart- the seventeen-year-old young man. He was buried here. Look at this – She is *Debri*, the beautiful wife of the lighthouse Superintendent Barkil. She got married in London and came to *Batighara* with dreams in her eyes. In the December of 1848, she closed her eyes to malaria. This is the tomb of lighthouse Superintendent Charles Fronary, and that's the tomb of the old light-keeper- James Laudon.

The light-keeper showed him/made him touch ten tombs and told him about them. He became emotional and said- Think about one thing. They came thousands of miles away from their country and stayed in this hot weather, marshy land, tiger-infested and accident-prone place to work here. It wasn't only about making money. They worked for the lighthouse, died here, and couldn't return to their country. They are resting in peace in the graveyard like a colony. They know that we are also working for the lighthouse, so they will cause no harm to us.

From that day onwards, while crossing the graveyard, he was never scared of the ghosts or the cemetery. Of course, while crossing the place at night, he walks faster to cross the cemetery and reach *Khubudhi* Colony. On the south of it is *the Dakshinakhala* Colony, and on the north is *Kajalpati* Colony. These places are tranquil at night. He reaches home through the dark passage. He could see the dim lights from the lantern and his child and wife sleeping. He could hear the deep breaths taken by his ailing mother in that silence of the night. On arrival, he washes his hands and legs and enters the kitchen. He warms the milk for the baby, cooks rice, cuts the vegetables, and prepares mixed vegetable curry. With the smell of the curry, his wife would get up from sleep and come to him. He would mix the rice and curry in a bowl and enter the mother's room to wake her up for food- 'Mother, get up and have rice.' He lifts his mother from the bed to make her sit and feeds her like a kid. If she cannot swallow the food, he would give her some water first and finally give her medicines. Some other times, he would apply warm mustard oil on both her feet. She would often cry like a baby, lift her hand slowly, and touch her throat. She tries to say something he can hardly comprehend and find out what she wants.

His mother is paralyzed from one side. She could only move one of her hands and try to convey what she intends through her eyes; sometimes, he can comprehend and often fails to do so. Once, his brother had a bitter cry, and she winked, then closed her mouth in one hand. He asked-'Mother, who tries to strangle you? Who closes your eyes? Who is that person? About whom are you saying?' His mother tries to say many things in her language, and he also tries to understand them. At that moment, his wife would call from the kitchen and say-' The rice is getting cold.' His mother would hold his hands and then push him away!

He sits near the plate for the dinner. He likes what he cooks. In the afternoons, as he feels hungry, he eats food even though he doesn't like it, but at night, he cooks by himself and enjoys his food. They take two sides on the bed, and the kid sleeps in the middle between them. One day, he asked her –'What is that mark on mother's throat? Why is she saying that her mouth and eyes were closed?'. Hearing this, his wife immediately replied-' In this house, we are only living with her. Who will do this? The old lady has become insane. She is having nightmares and uttering nonsense.'

Does his paralytic mother think of the nightmares as possibilities and cries, or is he incapable of inferring the truth? Very often, he needs answers to these questions. He would get up from the bed and pace up and down in the courtyard for some time. The light from the lighthouse would flash on his face.

He imagines it as if there is no light from the moon and stars near the lighthouse. At night, he could hear the noise from her sleeping mother, which would make him attentive. How old was he? He was hardly fourteen to fifteen months old baby when his mother died, and his father again got married in *Jambu* and brought a stepmother. She treated him like her son and took good care of him. His father was very meek and mild, whereas his mother was dominating. He grew up in an environment where his mother kept a warm relationship and deeper bonding with other *Bangladeshi* refugees and *Odias*. She married his stepson to her aunt's daughter's daughter (!) from *Baulakani* village. After his father's demise, she requested people to give him a job in the lighthouse. She is also like a lighthouse. Her mother and the lighthouse stood in a place but enlightened others' lives. Mother should live longer. He feels restless- His mother needs food with more vitamins and medicines, but he doesn't have enough money to purchase them.

He would sleep at home only for two to three hours. He has to get up early in the morning as the fowl starts howling and completes his daily chores. He fries white flour and adds water, sugar and salt to make dough. He would wake his mother to brush, help her wash her face for ablution and then make her eat the fried wheat flour. He would give her medicine, eat some fried wheat dough, and move towards the lighthouse.

He feels like a world full of joy and happiness whenever he enters the lighthouse compound. The lighthouse stands before him, like a tall man wearing a shirt with white and saffron strips and a star signing on the chest. Next to it was the double-storied rest house building, and on the other side was the switch room and the pole to show direction. A few dilapidated officer's quarters stand next to the lighthouse as they were out of use for extended periods. In front of the gate lies a road leading to the marshy forest. The wind blowing from the river and sea always rejuvenates him.

He starts morning duty by opening the lighthouse door and climbing the stairs to reach the balcony. He forgets all the woes of the world after reaching the top. To avoid entry into the sunlight, he opens those long curtains in the lantern room. The light keeper had told him –'It's necessary to hang the curtains there, and if the curtains aren't hung, then the prisms will get spoilt because of the sunlight.' In between, the light keeper checks everything and enters the lantern room. He then fixes the bulbs.

After drawing the curtains, he wanted to go out, but the light-keeper stopped him and asked to clean the lantern room. He said –'Clean all the available brass seals properly. These seals are from 'Schakonate Company', and whatever instruments you see in the lantern room belong to the same company. They are manufactured in London and are almost hundred and eighty years old. These instruments have helped in the functioning of the lighthouse. The *False Point* light is the only lighthouse in the world where the wick burns for a week continuously.'

The light-keeper often says- 'The lighthouse is like a mother. It keeps an eye on everyone. One-third of the earth is covered with water; the vehicles run on land, but the lighthouse shows the direction at night to the steamers, boats, and submarines, which carry thousands of people. Every year, one or two lighthouses are being built in different places. Even a lighthouse is there in the desert. The lighthouse workers travel there by helicopter. The wicks burning in the lighthouse's lantern room are like its eyes. Do you know how carefully they are made?'

He nodded his head as he didn't know this before. The light keeper told about the wick in the lantern room. He said, 'The lighthouse was lighted using an air brake for the first time. With the help of two narrow pipes, the oil (kept under the water) rose one hundred and forty meters up with air pressure to the lantern room. The labourer struggled throughout the night and turned on the turbine. After this, the lighthouse General called Engineer Stephenson from Scotland to this lighthouse. Stephenson saw the lighthouse running on air brake and said the light was too dim. If its capacity can be increased, then the light can be seen till Mahanadi delta's '*False Point*', which can guide the boats that far. Then only *the Hamerchance Brothers* company arrived. The company replaced the six-wick capillary with an 85 mm petroleum vapour wick and installed the generator. In March. 1931, the wicks were ignited. The diesel generator supplied power to the room throughout the night. Because of this lighthouse, the *Batighara* area was provided electricity in 1958. Since that year, with the help of electricity and a generator, the lighthouse never stopped functioning. It has never been in darkness since 1838, though the wick was often changed in the lantern room. Its life is light, and we must keep the wick burning for the light.

The lighthouse keeper always talks about responsibility and duty. Most often, both of them climb down the stairs. He waters the plants in the lighthouse front garden. He runs to the grocery shop to purchase groceries for the light keeper, sometimes carries the key to his house to open it and sits on his torn, old sofa. Sometimes, he eats some mixture and biscuit kept in the place, drinks water from his filter, fills the water tub in the bathroom, grinds mustard and garlic, and returns the house keys to the light-keeper, who, most of the time, sits and talks with the daily wage earning, lady sweeper.

When he returned home, he couldn't find his wife. After finishing cooking, his wife eats food and then goes with the baby to the neighbour's house to play cards or watch television. He would take some rice and curry to feed his mother.

On that day, when he glanced at Mother's face, he was surprised as one side of her cheek had turned purple. He asked-' Mother, what is this mark on your face? Did anyone beat you?'

His mother wasn't in a condition to tell him anything. He could only see tears in her eyes. He fed his mother, washed her mouth, and made her lie down on the bed and asked politely-' I wouldn't say anyone anything. Tell me who has slapped you?'

His mother shut her mouth with one hand and kept the rug on her face. He shouted and called his wife. His wife, who was playing cards in the neighbour's house, came running with the baby and asked-'What happened?' He pushed her into the dark room, removed the rug from her mother's face, and asked, 'What is this?' His wife laughed and said-' Maybe it's an insect bite. I will get some coconut oil to apply to it. Why are you creating such a noisy fuss for such a small matter?'

The visitors must have gathered near the lighthouse for the ticket by this time. Why is there a mark on his mother's face? Was it the mark of a slap or an insect bite? He couldn't find an answer to his questions. He ate quickly and left for the lighthouse. He took the ticket receipt book from the switch room and sat on the concrete bench. Visitors started purchasing the tickets. He learned there was no provision for the visitors to enter the lighthouse during British rule. The family members of the lighthouse workers and school children were only allowed to visit the lighthouse. Post-British rule, a provision was made to get a ticket by paying ten *paisa* to go and stand on the balcony of the lighthouse. Ten *paisa* has now increased to ten rupees for an entry into the lighthouse. He collects money, gives the tickets, and stands at the lighthouse's door as a ticket checker. He cautions the visitors: ' Don't touch anything in the lantern room, and then allow them to enter the lighthouse.'

The signalman enters the switch room after the visitors climb the lighthouse stairs. A few old people who couldn't climb the stairs sit on the concrete bench in the open area. They looked at their family members standing on the lighthouse's balcony. The signalman comes to that place and speaks to those old people. He asks-' Do you know about the king of *Kujanga*?' The visitors respond- *Kujanga's* king *Bidyadhara*? The king is playing an insane game. Suppose he knows that in the nearby village, any woman Will deliver in a few days. He will send his soldiers to bring that woman forcibly in that case. He sits on a chair in a lonely place along with his people and ties the woman with her legs apart. When she gets labour pain and gives birth to the child, this idiot king will clap and feel happy. Are you asking about that king?'

-'Yes, it's about that *Kujanga* King.' The signalman says- this is where the king of *Kujanga* came for hunting. Earlier, the name of this place was *Kaudia* Island. This place had marshy forests, rivers, and canals and was a deserted land filled with wild animals. This is somewhere around 1835 when the British government thought that near *Mahanadi* delta was a *False Point*, where many boats crash-landed and sank while going to Hooghly port. Many lives were lost due to these accidents. So, they felt it necessary to construct a lighthouse here. The Chief Engineer from *Kolkata*, Richard Lion, came here and surveyed this place. In the year 1867, the construction work started. Big boats and smaller ships carried boulders from *Barabati* Fort at *Cuttack* through *the Kendrapada- Marsaghai* canal came here. The lighthouse was constructed with a base of ten feet as its circumference. In March 1838, for the first time, the lighthouse was powered by Engineer H. Raiel. Like insects fly towards the light, people from *Ramnagar, Baulakani, Mahakalpada, Jambu,* and people staying on the other side of river *Kharnasi* started visiting this island to see the lighthouse. First, the *Odias* and *Maedinpur Bengalis* occupied this land parcel. Afterwards, they started selling their land to the *Bangladeshi* refugees at throw-away prices. Slowly, the site was inhabited by *Bangladeshi* refugees. The *Odia* people only named the lighthouse area –*Batighara.*

The old people were no longer interested in listening to the signalman's stories. They wanted to return home before sunset. At that time, the visitors would climb down from the lighthouse. The light keeper also would reach there to collect money and switch on the lights. He would climb the lighthouse to pull out the curtains to clean the lantern room, and after that, he would stand on the balcony. From the top of the lighthouse, the cyclone shelter, *Anganwadi Kendra,* and the small market looked like toys. In between, the light keeper would switch on the light, and the flash in the lantern room would reflect on his eyes. He then would close the lantern room door, lock it, close the lighthouse door, and reach the switch room. In that twilight, the lightkeeper and the signalman were busy talking to each other. The light keeper would tell him about scary things. He would say–' At night, never climb the lighthouse and go to its balcony. If someone goes there alone at night, he will either faint or commit suicide by jumping from atop.'

The signalman laughs at the light keeper's statement. The light keeper will argue and say–' In *Odisha,* this is *False Point* lighthouse. Other lighthouses exist at *Puri, Konark,*

Gopalpur, and *Paradeep*; similar incidents also happen there. All over the world, wherever there is a lighthouse, there are plenty of stories like this.

The signalman said-' Are you mad? How can one faint and jump from the lighthouse if he climbs it at night?' The light keeper will argue to prove his point and say-' A man isn't insane right from the beginning. But when he reaches a high place alone, he remembers all his past problems of life and turns insane.'

-' It might be happening in the lighthouse without watchmen. Our lighthouse doesn't have a record of such incidents.' The signalman always waits for an opportunity to confront the light keeper.

These two lighthouse workers are always ready to argue with each other. The light keeper is an employee of *Bengal Boat Company*, and the signalman is an employee of the *Government of Odisha*. Both of them were jealous of each other. They stay separately in their quarters and sometimes take leave to visit their family. Whenever they don't have work, they sit together, discuss many things, and end up arguing with each other. He heard from the signalman that in 1875, around forty employees in the lighthouse stayed with their families in the crowded colony. There was a head light keeper, four light keepers, a peon, a sweeper, a doctor, a washer man, a barber, coolie, and a boatman. The lighthouse family was big by including their family members. By 1970, the number had reduced to only 23. At present, there are only two in the lighthouse. Only two people can become friends in a lonely place or can argue with each other. He left them in their own world and hurriedly walked towards his house.

One day, while returning home at night, he saw

someone running towards him with a torchlight. It was his nephew who lived with him in the colony. He had come to give him the news about the death of his mother. There were a few women from the neighbourhood who had assembled there. He could hear the crying of his child and wife in the house. When he entered the house, his wife saw him and started crying loudly. She yelled-' Why did you leave me and go, mother? I looked after you like my mother. You left me alone, Mother. I am the daughter-in-law. How will I manage the house without you?'

He wasn't in a mood to listen to his wife's words. He ran into the room where his mother was lying. Her face was covered by a rug. He took out the carpet and looked at his mother's face. Her eyes had bulged out, mouth wide, and she was lifeless.

He controlled his emotions, told his wife to keep quiet, and asked her with suspicion-' I came and fed mother, gave her medicine in the afternoon. She was fine at that time. How did she die? What happened to her suddenly?'

With tears in his eyes, he stood beside his mother with many questions. His wife continuously cried and said,' I am ill-fated. I didn't know about it. I was busy playing cards and watching television. My child was also not well, and when I came to light the lamp in the evening, I saw that mother was no more. She was suffering from disease; only God knows how she died.'

He couldn't convince himself with what he heard from his wife. He could see his dead mother's wide-open eyes looking at him. He forgot to question further and realized the last rites must be performed. A pit was dug in one corner of his compound, and according to *Vaishnava* rituals, the body was washed, dressed in fresh cloth, and bedecked with flowers. The dead body was then placed on the pit in a sitting position, covered with a piece of cloth, and the pit was covered with soil.

The next day in the morning, he went to the lighthouse and sobbed in front of the lightkeeper and said-'After his mother's death, stepmother took care of him. She managed the house when there was a problem with the *Odia* refugees. She got him married and also arranged for his job in the lighthouse.' He was nostalgic as he remembered the bygone days.

The light keeper tried to console him by singing *Baul Sangeet*- 'Your mother died now, your father died before, then you will go, and your child will follow. The world is like a play. You can see the graveyard here. You can see the tomb of *Debra*, wife of the head light keeper *Mr. Barkil*. Mr *Barkil* broke his leg here, went to *Puri* for treatment, and lost his life there. His dead body couldn't reach here as the body sank into the sea and was lost. There was another higher official of the lighthouse, *Mr. Barnard*, and his colleague, *Mr. Spooner*. The boat sank midway in the river from *Kujanga* to *Batighara*, and their dead bodies were never found. Many people working in the lighthouse died as they were drowned while travelling by boat. In the year 1871, there was a super-cyclone. The boat *'Veldha'*, carrying food grains, eatables, sugar, and wine, sank near the *False Point* in *Hukitola*. Many dead bodies were seen floating on water. Many people have died due to the tiger's attack, malaria, and drowning. But isn't our lighthouse still standing like a hero for a zillion years in this mortal world? Try to understand that human life is concise and finite compared to the life of the lighthouse. We will also perish one day by working in the lighthouse.'

He asked the light keeper to sanction him leave for thirteen days to complete the rituals. He also asked for some advance amount. The light keeper tried to make him understand- 'This lighthouse is our source of living. We have to work here. If you take thirteen days' leave, will you get the wage for those thirteen days? Take leave only for five days. The first two days and the last three days to complete the rituals. Come this evening and pull the curtains of the lantern room; at that time, we will consider the advance amount.'

He wiped his tears and nodded his head. He had a lot of responsibility now. He crossed river *Kharnasi* and gave the message to his relatives' house at *Ramnagar* and to other friends. He gave the letter to his in-law's house in *Baulakani*, crossed the river *Gobari* and informed in his uncle's house. After completion of the rituals, the relatives left the place. The next day, he went and stood on the lighthouse's balcony. Whenever he climbs up, he looks at his house in the village, but he can never locate it properly because of the trees. He thought- There were people in the place except for his mother. He still couldn't forget his mother's face, with eyes bulging out. He became restless and apprehensive. Diverse thoughts intertwined through his mind.

The next day, he fished his work quickly, crossed the river, went to *Ramnagar* to meet a locksmith and made two duplicate keys of the lighthouse. After his mother's demise, all of them were scared to enter the room where his mother died. He slept on his bed, and at midnight, he woke up and called his wife. He spoke to her sweetly and said-' After Mother's death, how will we live in this house. I will go to the lighthouse for work, and you will be busy playing cards and watching television. How will the house be managed?'

Both husband and wife hadn't spoken to each other for almost a month by then, but he talked to his wife softly that night. She felt happy and said, 'As the old lady was in the house, I went out to play cards and watch television. Now everything will be fine. I will join *Mahila Mandal* and will get a television at our home. I will not go to anyone's house and take care of my house. You will see the difference in how the house was maintained when your mother was alive and now.'

-' OK, we will do everything, but I want to ask you something before that. When can I ask?' His wife was surprised to hear this statement. He tried to ease the situation and said-' Let us go to the lighthouse and discuss there.'

-' What will you ask me before the light keeper and the signalman? He immediately replied to clarify her doubt and said-' We will climb the lighthouse at night to reach the balcony and talk there.' His wife had never visited the lighthouse. She was thrilled and asked- 'Will you take me there and to the lantern room? He said- 'Oh Yes, I will take you there. You will climb those hundred and forty steps to reach the balcony.' His wife was thrilled and said- Let me finish the cooking early so we can go.'

The next day, till the evening, he was busy with the visitors cleaning the lantern. The light keeper switched on the light, and the morning started flashing immediately. He quickly completed the daily chores in the light keeper's house and returned home. He was surprised that his wife had cleaned and decorated the house nicely. She had already finished cooking and feeding the baby, and the baby was sleeping. Wearing a good saree, she was waiting for him.

His wife talked continuously while he finished his

supper. She spoke about the quarrel in the neighbour's house. She said she had pain in her left chest and wanted to go to *Ramnagar* Hospital. She also wanted to visit her sister's *Paradeep* house during *Viswakarma Puja*. He was busy eating his dinner and said yes to everything. His wife went to the pond to clean the utensils. He paced up and down in the courtyard as he was feeling restless. He called her up and said-'Let's go.' His wife was surprised and asked -'At night?' He said firmly-'Yes, tonight.' His wife asked-'What about the child?' He said- let the child sleep in the house. We will go there and return quickly.'

They left their home and cautiously walked towards the lighthouse. The dogs started barking on the way. There was nobody in the lighthouse compound. The light keeper and the signalman were already sleeping in their quarters. While walking towards the lighthouse, he felt he wasn't going to the lighthouse but to an unknown place with his wife. He opened the gate with the duplicate key he made in *Ramnagar*, opened the lighthouse door, indicated his wife towards the spiral staircase, and said,' Let's go and climb it.'

He remembered what the light keeper had said: 'If someone goes to the top of the lighthouse at night, then he will either become insane or will jump and commit suicide.'

Reaching the balcony, he could feel the soft wind blowing and see the shadows of the trees in the darkness and the fireflies around them. He could hear the chirping of the birds at night. That night was total silence as if no one but two existed. His wife was going around the balcony. When his wife looked down from the balcony excitedly, he called her and said-' I want to ask you something. How did my mother die? My mother showed me the marks on her throat and cheek. She didn't blame anyone and kept quiet. Who gave her so much pain during her death that her eyes bulged out? In our house, only we are there. Who else can do all these other than you?' He became furious, started beating his wife, then caught her by the neck, lifted her in the air, and said- 'you have killed my mother. You wanted her to die. Didn't you kill my mother? Tell me the truth, or I will throw you down from this lighthouse, and then I will jump from the lighthouse.'

His wife was scared, looked at him in horror, and felt as if her heartbeat was going to stop. He didn't care about it. He tried to pull his wife towards the edge of the balcony, and she tried to escape from his clutches, and as his hold was a little loose, she slipped. She fell on the floor, held his feet, and said- I have done the sin. Hand me over to the police, but don't kill me and kill yourself. Just think once about our little child sleeping alone at home. Pardon me. Please pardon me.'

He thought about his innocent child sleeping alone at home, and suddenly, his annoyance burst like a bubble. His decision to throw his wife from the balcony changed immediately. He freed himself from the hands of his wife and said-'Go down'.

CHAPTER-7

Once the lights are switched off from the Batighara- Life starts- at fishing jetty, river bank and in the market. There is a day's crowd in the market of life. AT home, in the colony, and in the market, there is an easier chaos of one's own language. One has to live a life of myriad colours- in and around the town.

Ramnagar was in sleep.

He was awake.

He was inside his low, thatched roof house, with a high rising platform, on the bed with a mosquito net. He sleeps outside daily for all the twelve months of the year; rest others are inside the house. He has a sense of pride being on the front *veranda* as this reflects his family headship. He says- what else is family headship? He is nothing more than a watchman. He has studied till Matric and sometimes scolds with a mix of *Bengali* and English. The young lads of *Ramnagar* don't give a damn to his words and take him lightly.

Till midnight, there is continuous chattering from the rats and his phonetic of *hes hes* that fills the air. He slaps on own face to kill the mosquitos that have entered through the holes in the mosquito net. There must be an hour or so still to be the dawn- a fistful of cold breeze from the sea side *Ramchandi* temple spread over the bed of Kharsanai like a supressed whisper. How many hours does he sleep actually? When people start roaming on the *Ramnagar* road with their gossips and with blowing of the vehicle horns he gets up; bowing down, sweeps the courtyard with a broom. He completes his daily chores. He eats a little bit and moves to *Ramnagar* marketplace and on arrival opens up his aluminium utensils shop shutter. He cleans the shop, does the puja, and sits in the corner of the shop to wait for arrival of the customers. With growing demand for steel utensils, why will people purchase aluminium utensils? Still, the demand for giant aluminium cauldrons, buckets, and iron pans have not gone down. Sometimes, he could sell one to two pieces to get handsome profit out of it. But most of the time, he sits in the shop without customers and he gazes at the crowded market in *Ramnagar* in awe.

Like a dream he remembers the year 1963. At that time, *Ramnagar* was a jungle and full of rivers, ravines and canals. There were crocodiles and alligators in the river water. There was a small temple of the goddess *Dariya Ramchandi* under a tree. There were cattle sheds for the Odiya cow herders. They were the original inhabitants of this place. Slowly, the refugees started settling here and there in clusters of three to five huts which grew into a village. There were nearly four to five hundred *Bangladeshi* families. A foot trail was from *Jambu*'s Chapali Square to *Ramnagar*, *Kharnasi* River, and *Batighara*. On both sides of the path was the marshy forest. There was a pan shop, a tea stall, and a tiffin stall for the refugees. Except for the morning and afternoons, as the day progresses, the road leading to *Batighara* will be deserted and appear lonely.

It was difficult to earn a living with family in this forest like area. He remembered when he carried the utensils in his bicycle and went to these small villages to sell. He also remembers- What did his father bring from *Bangladesh*? He left his high yielding fields, coconut orchards and home to arrive at *Kolkata*. He had only a few clothes, utensils, and some silver jewellery. It took a lot of work for him to manage the house they rented in 24 *Parganas*. His father's elder brother arrived at *Ramnagar* and found it perfect to stay there and start a business. He had five hundred rupees with him. A refugee who got one-acre land from the government; had built a home and a pond wanted to sell his property so that he could go and live with his relatives in *Sundarbans*. First he made him god-brother and told that person – 'Sell your property to us as we belong to the same caste and have come from the same place, *Khulna* in *East Bengal*. That means one family will sell the property to the other family.'

The refugee said- land, pond, and the orchards along with one acre of land will cost not less than two hundred rupees.'

He said-'I will give hundred and fifty rupees.' He bargained with him like a trader. The refugees reduced ten rupees and said- hundred and ninety rupees.' He re-bargained and brought down the offer further- ' Give for a hundred and eighty rupees.' As the landowners are always greedy, the refugee showed the last bit of his false pride and said-' Give another one rupee.' The deal was finalized for a hundred and eighty-one rupees for one acre of land and building.

In a shop devoid of customers, he sits down and calculates the worth of his property. The land he has near the road to *Ramnagar* is valued at fifty lakhs rupees per *guntha*. He has constructed six shops on the plot and given it on rent. One shop is for him where he sells aluminium utensils. At the backside of the shop is his residence with a big courtyard. There are a few thatched roof rooms, four kitchens, a toilet, a tube well, and a barn in the court yard. He has four sons and a daughter who are married to wealthy families. Whoever gets married is allocated a separate residence. Further to his market complex, starts the crowded, noisy marketplace of *Ramnagar*. Among those crowded thatched roof properties lives his dynastic family.

In 1963, with only five hundred rupees in the pocket. it was terrifying for him to stay in that forest infested with thieves and dacoits.

Slowly around *Ramnagar* other villages like *Barajbahapur, Pitapata, Uttarpada, Sharkarpada* emerged with the people from *Nuakhali, Baisala, Haritpur, Dhaka, Chatgram, Khulna, and Patuala* of East Bengal. People with designations like *Chakraborty, Ghosh, Burman, Rai, Guha, Mondal, Mitra, Das, Biswas, Jhali, and Sarkar* were among them.

In 1971, the country was divided into Pakistan and *East Bengal*. Then, many people from *Bangladesh* sold their property in throw away prices and were flushed with cash when they arrived at *Ramnagar*. A few sold the allotted properties they got as refugees in *Malkangiri* and *Koraput* and came down to *Ramnagar* to live forever. The farmers and small businessmen from *East Bengal* sold their properties there and came to *Ramnagar* started some or other businesses. They made small boats here and started fishing. The fishery business boomed. The fishing business encroached everyone- the fish platform owners, fishnet owners, fishing labours, the fish jetty, ice factory and people earned made tons of money. The *Ramnagar* market was overly crowded with lights in the evening as there was plenty of cash floating around from the sea fishing business. Many cloth stores, medicine shops, tailor shops, shoe stores, ladies' corners, grocery shops, hotels, and tiffin centres existed. People crowded in front of the chat *golgapa* stalls and fast food centres. They spoke in *Bengali* in the market, and the *Bengali* songs were in the music systems. He felt as if *Ramnagar* was a mini *Bangladesh*, and he was happy.

But his wife was growing old and was unhappy. She was from *Kharnasi*. She wasn't able to dominate her daughter-in-law. She spent most of her time with elder daughter -so the other three daughters-in-law were unhappy with her. He and his wife take lunch in all four sons' houses in turns so his wife doesn't have the responsibility of cooking. As there were five ladies in the house, there was always a quarrel between them. The third daughter-in-law purposely uses the word-'Thief'. The second daughter in law says that she gives everything to her daughter. His wife would cry and leave for her daughter's house, and would stay there for fifteen to twenty days. Then she starts thinking about her husband and returns back to again to *Ramnagar*. At night, after dinner, his wife comes to his bed with medicine and a glass of water. Sometimes, he holds her hand and makes her to sit close to him. His wife would feel shy and try to run away from there by saying-' You are a shameless man. You don't have any iota of shame left in you. There are grandchildren in the house who are pretty grown up.' She goes away and closes her room door. He smiles and thinks that she will come again with the medicine and water tomorrow. He doesn't feel good whenever his wife isn't at home, though other family members are around. He thinks that if she isn't happy with the daughter-in-law at this age and wants to stay with her daughter, then let her go. He is alone on his bed at this age. He recalls *Ravindra Nath Tagore's* song – *Jadi Kae Tor Dak* (If no one is listening to your call out) … and sings to himself to feel better.

When there are no customers in the shop, he would have stray thoughts and doze off with his mouth open and saliva dropping from it (!).

While he was immersed in these thoughts, a customer came to the shop. He sat upright. The customer selected a giant cauldron to purchase. He calculated the price as per the kilogram and quoted. The customer said-' In *Kendrapada* and *Cuttack*, the cost is two hundred rupees per kilogram for aluminium utensils. Why are you charging so much?'

- 'This is *Kolkata's Bahubazar's* item. Its price is lesser than *Cuttack*. You don't know that the price has increased a lot. This utensil costs two hundred and fifty rupees in *Cuttack*; at *Kolkata*, it's two hundred and forty.'

- 'Will you take whatever you say?' The customer asked. He was in a hurry to sell. He said-' Give me only ten rupees more from the purchase price. I can't sell less than that.' The customer was annoyed by listening to him.

He said-' All the businessmen in *Ramnagar* and those who are wealthy are illegal migrants. How do you know how a poor customer lives here? You are all worried about your profit.'

He felt humiliated after listening to the rude customer. He was agitated within and said-'What are you saying? Am I an illegal migrant? This is your wrong notion. I was born in *Kolkata's* 24 *Praganaa*. I have completed my Matric from *Radha Bhalab High School*. I am born in this country-How can I be an illegal migrant?'

-What about your father and grandfather? Were they not illegal migrants?'

The customer left without purchasing anything, but his words echoed and pierced through his heart. In that pain, he uttered the word *Maa* (Mother) and recalled the goddess *Daria Ramchandi*. After a while he was normal. The goddess *Daria Ramchadi* resides in everybody's faith. *Daria Ramchandi* is believed to be the sister of *Puri Ramchandi*. When *Kalapahad* started destroying the Hindu temples, *Maa Ramchandi* came here and emerged beneath a *Neem* tree. She appeared in the dreams of a priest and said-'Worship me and let people know about my glory'. Whenever the fishermen or the boatmen take their boat in the river, they pray *Maa Daria Ramchandi* and plead with her to protect them.

The *Daria Ramchandi*'s temple has a proper boundary, a *kirtan* (prayer) room, a kitchen, a rest house for the devotees, and a toilet. Many devotees flung into the temple every day. Many festivals are celebrated in the temple, and people perform the marriage ceremony and oblation. The shops in front of the temple were always crowded.

He was a little restless. He thought he would close the shop, go to the temple, and convey his worries to *Maa Ramchandi*. Will mother goddess answer his prayers? The priests in the temple don't pay attention to the devotees without any honorarium. Why will they listen to him? At that time, he wanted someone to listen to him. After he started following *Shri Shri Thakur Anukul Chandra*, he stopped going frequently to *Daria Ramchandi* temple. After visiting *Thakur Anukul Chandra's Satsang*, he has developed compassion and a liking for fellow human beings. At that moment, he remembered about a person- *Mukul Da- Mukul Kishore Raisharma*.

In the evening, he closed the shop, crossed *Ramnagar* market, and went to the temple of *Shri Anukul Chandra*. His ears were resounding with the words which the customer said. He knows that the customer is a refugee and belongs to *Uttarpada*. He works in the fishery company's boat as a labourer. They earn a lot of money because of the fishing business, so they are quite adamant. He knows about the nature of the refugees who have settled here. All of them have refugee cards, and they have got the land from the government without paying anything. When *Nalini Mohanty* was an MLA, their names were entered in the voter's list, and at that time, they got one acre of land per head. The refugees, those who got an acre of land per head, have divided the land among their children, and now they have at least got one *guntha* to one and a half *guntha* with each of them. They couldn't prosper by fishing, working as labourers, and doing small business. Right from the beginning, they were lazy in terms of earning money. They believe in making and spending on the same day. Among them, many are illiterate, and there is always a problem of scarcity of money in these family.

According to them, the *East Bengal* people who have come with the money are illegal migrants. They are doing their business with the money they earned in *East Bengal*. They are spreading their business and also have the politicians along with them to help them. That's why there is always an argument between the refugees and the prosperous migrants. They feel that if they make a mockery of these successful people, then the credit is theirs. But he couldn't easily digest the parody.

He climbed the stairs of *Thakur Anukul Chandra's* temple and entered the marble hall. In the temple, on the pedestal were the photos of *Shree Shree Anukula Chandra,* his guru *Hajur Maharaj,* his wife *Sarashibala Devi, Shree Shree Bada Maa,* his elder son *Amarendranath Chakrabarty,* and *Shree Shree Bada Da.* By that time, both the evening *kirtan* and puja were already over. The place had a sweet smell of flowers. He bowed in front of the photos, sat in the hall, looked at the picture of *Shri Shri Anukul Chandra,* and waited eagerly for *Mukul Da.*

Thakur Ankul Chandra was born in *Himayetpur in the Sandalya Gotra, Chakravarty* family, and was *Kanyakubja* Brahmin. He was studying MBBS in *Kolkata's Bahubazar* National Medical School but wasn't interested to pursue the profession. He was inclined towards spirituality and *Satsang.* That was the time when the country was divided into two parts- India and Pakistan, he realized that it would be difficult for him to conduct *Satsang* in a Muslim-occupied place. He fell sick, and the doctors advised a change of place so that his health would improve. In 1946, the Thakur family shifted from *East Bengal* to Bihar's *Deoghar,* where the *Santal* tribal lived. In the family, *Shree Shree Thakur, Bada Maa, Bada Da, Chota* Da, and his grandsons started the propagation of the concept of *'Satsang Guru bhai'* and built temples worldwide. There are beautiful temples at *Kendrapada* and *Ramnagar.* In *Jambu, Ramnagar,* and *Kharnasi,* many of them turned followers of *Shree Shree Thakur* and became *Guru Bhai* (religious brother under the same master). Eating food prepared without onion and garlic, keeping aside some money to donate to the temple every day, spending life as per the order, and meeting *Guru bhai* during the birthday celebration of *Shree Shree Thakur, Bada Maa, Bada*

Da brought immense pleasure in life. The temples became the most sacred and pious place for many.

When he was thinking about all this, *Mukul Da* came. He asked-' What happened? How are you? You are here after so many days. You don't come for the *Satsang* very often.'

He was in a hurry to narrate the incident with him to *Mukul Da*. *Mukul Da* suddenly went from there to draw the hall curtains to close the temple. When the Hindu-Muslim riot was going on, *Mukul Da's* family left *East Bengal* and came by a fast moving train from *Dhaka* that touched the wind speed of 100-150 miles/hour. They reached *Kolkata's Howrah* station. They didn't bring anything with them and took shelter in *Howrah* station. They begged in the *Howrah* station platform and did petty jobs to earn their living. The children of the family members were born on the railway platform and grew up there. *Mukul Da's* father thought they would spend their entire life in the station and, finally, die there; otherwise, they would go to any other station by train. In the meantime, *Mukul Da's* family got a refugee card. Back then, there were refugee camps in *Odisha's Koraput, Malkanagiri, Charbatia, and Bhadrakh's Maitarapur*. They got the land from the government in *Bhadrakh's Baidapur station's Maitrapur* and settled there. *Mukul Da* was born in *Maitarapur*. *Mukul Da's* father, *Ramlal Rai*, was a *Guru bhai in the Satsang*. Once, he visited *Ramnagar* for some *Satsang* work and saw that many refugees from East Bengal had settled there. *Ramnagar* was a refugee town. He thought he could do some small business there and expand the work of *Satsang*. So, they sold their land in *Maitrapur* and shifted to *Kharnasi*. After his father's death, *Mukul Da* got involved in *Satsang's* work. The renowned *Guru bhais* of the *Satsang* conferred the *Brahmins* with different titles. *Mukul Da* was conferred with the Sharma title.

Mukul Da says-' There are four types of Brahmins. If a *Brahmin* marries a *Khetriya*, he is called *Murdha Brahmin*. If the Brahmin gets married to a *Vaishya* girl, then he is called *Amrastha Brahmin*. The Brahmin who gets married to a *Sudra* girl is called *Parshik Brahmin*. *Mukul Da* was *Parshik Brahmin*. As *Parshik Brahmin*, *Mukul Da* took care of the *Satsang*, constructing the temple and arrangement of different celebrations. *Mukul Da* was dark and short. He wore a white kurta and always had a smile on his face. He asked him again what had happened? You are here at the wrong time.'

- '*Mukul Da*, please tell me if I am an illegal migrant? He conveyed his worries. *Mukul Da* asked-' What happened?'

- 'Today, a refugee boy of *Uttarpada* told me this. It was like a slap on my face. You know that I was born in *Kolkata's 24 Pragana* and I have completed my studies from the school there. This country is my mother. Am I an illegal migrant?'

Mukul Da could make out that *Mondal* was worried. He knew people couldn't easily digest the humiliation and live in pain. To console him, *Mukul Da* said- Listen! Thakur has said, "Whenever you get an instinct to find fault with others- at that time, the same fault dwells on you. If you don't waste your time and throw away that thought and instinct at the earliest, you can escape from it; otherwise, everything will be destroyed.'

- 'Why am I still in pain? Why am I feeling suffocated after listening to those words?'

- 'Grief is also a feeling, and so is happiness. Grief is the natural reaction of loss.' *Mukul Da* repeated the words of *Shree Shree Thakur*. But there is no end to humiliation in grief. He was anxious about a small question. He felt as if *Mukul Da* was very close to him, so he repeatedly uttered the same thing in an emotional tone. He said-' *Mukul Da*, you must know that my father came from *East Bengal* and stayed in *Kolkata*. If he is an illegal migrant, then as I am born in this country, then how can I be an illegal migrant?'

- 'You are your father's heir, so your father's actions impact you. Look! We are like the heir of *Shree Shree Ankul Chandra*; we are *Guru bhais*.'

- '*Mukul Da*, there is a hell and heaven difference between *Guru bhai* and illegal migrants.' He wasn't able to understand. He was annoyed and irritated. He was trying to put on his argument. *Mukul Da* became firm and thundered,' *Shree Shree Thakur* left *East Bengal* and stayed in *Bihar's Deoghar*. Is he not an illegal migrant? All the countries in the world have unlawful migrants. The people who have converted a forest or a desert into settlements are migrants. Let it be America or *Ramnagar*- People from outside are there in all the places. Remember one thing- 'A migrant crosses the border in that way, all the people of *Ramnagar* are migrants.'

In this world, all are migrants. Why are you in grief about it? He tried to make him convenient, but he wasn't convinced. He couldn't accept the argument from his heart. Finally, he bowed down in front of *Shree Shree Thakur* and was about to climb down the stairs when *Mukul Da* said what Shree Shree Thakur noted-' Follow the thoughts that are good for you'.

He was feeling lifeless as his conscience was pricked.

He strolled around. It was almost night then; the small shops in *Ramnagar* were closed, and a few big shops were about to close. *Khokan* standing near the tea shop, asked, 'why are you so late at night? Are you coming back from the temple?'

He nodded his head and walked. *Khokan* said-' Do you know uncle, *Ramnagar*, *Kharnasi*, and *Batighara* areas are declared as sanctuary. People will no longer stay here. Animals will stay here. This place is a sanctuary now.'

He didn't answer. As *Mukul Da* said, migrants are here and everywhere. All of those who are staying in *Ramnagar* are like animals. Which new animals will stay here?'

He couldn't enjoy his dinner. When he went to sleep on his bed, his elder son's daughter *Shiuli* brought the medicine and a glass of water. His wife had gone to daughter's house for almost twenty days. She had given her elder grandchild the responsibility of regularly providing him with medicine. He wanted to ask *Shiuli* the question running in his mind and finally asked-' Are you a migrant?'

- 'What do you mean? What are you saying- Migrant? I don't know the meaning of this.' She showed him the medicines he would take and hurriedly left the place to again get engrossed in her mobile world.

Few children like *Shiuli* passed matric because of a high school teacher. This teacher also told them he would help them pass plus two and kept them in a Sanskrit toll mess. *Shiuli* was wearing a dress which she bought from a mall in *Cuttack*. She speaks *Odia*, *Hindi*, and English, that needs further improvement. She feels ashamed of speaking in her mother tongue in front of outsiders. She often purchases mobile vouchers and stands near the fast food stall to eat *chowmin* with a fork. How will this new generation understand the meaning of migrant? His sons also ignored it. It is he only who thinks about this phenomenon.

He was almost half asleep and suddenly remembered about taking his medicine. The courtyard was filled with the moonlight. The water in the glass sparkled with the moonbeam.

He took out the medicine. The words still lingered in his mind. He forgot which medicine he was supposed to take, which one did *Shiuli* tell him. He took out a red round tablet, gulped it, and drank some water. After some time, he thought that the medicine he had taken is incorrect. He took out a black capsule, gulped it, and again drank some water. He thought that even this medication is also wrong. He took out a white and yellow pill from the polythene packet and gulped it.

He was awake all night. The people in *Ramnagar* were sleeping, but he was awake. The hatred and anger within made him apprehensive. He screamed and shouted loudly-'I am not an illegal migrant.' He became unconscious, and there was chaos in the family. He was shifted to the hospital by an auto rickshaw. A few refugees were on their way to work in the early morning. They saw him and said-' The miser who was an illegal migrant died!'

He was no more in a state to listen to all these. He was in the world of doctors, nurses, injections, and saline. In the hospital, near his bed, his wife stood with her daughter and son-in-law from *Kharnasi*, his sons, daughters-in-law, and grandchildren- everybody is an illegal migrant! Then there played an old musical tune in his mother tongue - You want to go? Where will you go? He smiled at himself.

CHAPTER-8

Where is his country amidst the thousands of settlements around the claimed aggregates? Which is his country- the nation he has left or where he has taken shelter? One country calls him – an emigrant. Another country weeds him out to call- a refugee. Until his death, a man never forgets that he is a citizen of the land where he was born.

He was short, fat, and had a protruding belly. He cleaned and fenced the boundary in front of his house like an artist. He was trying the fence with a nylon rope and continuously engaged in talking to himself.

- In the year 1971, there was a war.

- In 1977, *Nalini Mohanty* became the MLA. During this time and between 1992, only a few of us got the ration card.

When the thought about the ration card emerged within, he was drenched with sweat. It's also a challenging task to talk to oneself continuously. He wiped the effort with his towel tied around the waist. It was getting hotter.

Completing the fencing work, he climbed up to the river wall and sat near the shadows of the holed boat tied near river *Gobari*.

Sometimes, to get rid of laziness, he spreads his legs straight and sits upright in a yogic posture, similar to a yoga session on television. This much is his yoga; he also becomes restless and can't stop self-conversation during this time. He starts self-talking again.

Other than talking with himself, he doesn't like gossiping with others. He has a wife, son, daughter-in-law, and grandchildren in his house- he only speaks what is the bare minimum required. He doesn't question too much. To others, he answers with 'Yes' or 'No'. He spends most of the time speaking to himself and getting answers to his questions.

-In 1992, only a few people in *Jambu* Panchayat got their ration cards. Those who gave the ration card returned asking for votes. It was a big scene on the day the ration cards were distributed. After getting the ration card, people without documentary proof had no bounds on their happiness. Holding the ration cards, they thundered - 'We got our country. India is now our own country.'

-All those who didn't have a ration card till 2011- I am one of them- I don't have a ration card, so I don't have a country.

He started crying aloud, and a couple of birds feasting on the insects from the rotten boat got scared and flew away towards the *banni (Prosopis Cineraria)* tree. He would get up from the shadows of the broken ship and restart the unfinished, pending fencing work. Who and why should someone spend so much time in such a routine and regular work? Keeping aside his attention elsewhere, he tries to keep himself engaged with hand–eye coordination. And deep inside, like a bumblebee, the nation hums inside his head.

- In this *Jambu land*, whenever someone got a ration card, he told the Maedinpuria *Bengalis*- You have come here with *the Burdwan* land document. You are saying that you belong to this country and we are refugees. We also had our own country, which was washed away and taken away from us because of war, and we didn't have any land records. They show their ration card and say- We are Indians.

'Yes, those who have got the ration cards among us; how many have received it legally?' The school teacher has taken five hundred rupees to enter the name in the voter list. People from the other country have acres and acres of land here. How did they register the land in their name? From them, the RI has taken a bribe, a gift of fish and crabs, and he also had a good time with the ladies of the house to register the land illegally in their names. Rascals! To get the ground, do you have to sell your honour?

As he didn't have his ration card, he sometimes scolded others. He keeps talking about the country like a torn flute, and at that time, his wife comes running from inside and says in a disgruntled voice-' Stop talking about the country. One day, you will become insane by speaking to yourself and also make us insane. Come and have your food.'

He hurriedly returns from the country to the house and washes himself in the nearby swallow pond. He joins us for lunch. He dips his fingers in the fish curry juice prepared by his daughter-in-law, along with some rice.

Like a chameleon, his wife sits beside him with a hand fan. The daughter-in-law would be out then to gather water from the tube well. His wife, who is always on a fault-finding mission with the daughter-in-law, asks-' How has the girl from *Mahakalpada* prepared the fish curry?'

He would take a fistful of rice into his mouth and reply, It's OK.'

She asks, 'What do you mean by it's OK?' She says,' Will the cooking here be better than how we cook in the Khulna area? When we left that country and came here, I was only seven years old, but my mother had taught me to cook seventeen types of dishes before I left for your house. This girl is from *Mahakalpada* and would cook fish (pun intended)!'

He would be neither with his wife, who learnt cooking in the Khulna area, nor with the girl's cooking craft from *Mahakalpada*. Now, he couldn't differentiate the taste of the food as he was always engrossed in his thoughts about the country despite being at the lunch table.

Only when he is around her would she get annoyed and speak ill of the country related to 'Leave that topic about the country. Go and rest for some time on your bed. You are always standing in the hot sun and busy with unnecessary fencing work. What will happen if you get a sunstroke?'

This is when his wife will take a plea for health issues and take him away from the country into the resting bed. Despite the flow of many afternoons just like that, he lacks any sleep. While idling on the bed, two countries simultaneously enter his mind. Then, a fierce war starts within.

-Yes, should there have been a war in that country? No,

it happened only because of *Yahiya Khan*. After the war, the government, now called *Bangladesh*, was East Pakistan. The land was fertile, with intense farming and high yields. But Pakistan is a mountainous region of plateaus, infertile land where an inch of grass would not grow. That's why there was always an eye of Pakistan on *East Bengal*. Before the war, they said *East Bengal* belonged to Pakistan, so the official language would be Urdu. The other group said- *Bangla* is our mother tongue. The problem started with language issues. They knew that there were many Hindus in *East Bengal who were* innocent, and if they robbed and killed the Hindus, they would be scared and leave *East Bengal*, and then they could enjoy the property. In the name of the Language Movement, many miscreants entered the villages.

He has heard that during 1947, these people had sent train loads filled with hacked breasts of Hindu women to India. He has heard about this fear of prestige from his father. Then, the country was heading towards war. Father said- get up, let's leave the country. Those were summer months (*Baisakh*), full moon nights. The unmarried aunt was crying, and so was the mother. I couldn't comprehend anything. I was hardly thirteen to fourteen years old and could not understand anything. I thought that we were going to another country to meet our relatives. Maybe there is a fair there, and after the fair, we will return to our own country. We boarded the boat at night, and the next day, we reached a new place. My father made me recognize the country, saying- 'This is India.'

- Is there any end to our struggle in this country? At *Jambu*, we cleaned the marshy forest and made huts for ourselves to stay in, and in 1971, there was a cyclone. Jamu was flooded with water from the river. Thirteen hundred and thirty-six people who had left East Bengal and taken sheltered here lost their lives. That incessant rain! The wind was blowing at a speed of hundred and fifty kilometres per hour. They kept us in a school building constructed during British rule. The cyclone came and passed through. We could survive in this country. My father again built the house. We survived eating crabs and fishes. After living in this country for two years, my uncle told my father- 'Brother, let's return to our country. We have our land and property there, so let's go. Let's go back to *Bangladesh*.' My father said- 'I have left the country, so I will never return there.'

Nobody has any say in his daily, routine chores about the country. In the beginning, his grandchildren showed interest. They listened to his stories, but gradually, they also lost their appeal and were busy playing some other games. Sometimes, the grandchildren sleep near him. He would caress two of his grandchildren, drawing them close to him, and say- Your father is borne here. Your mother belongs to this country, so you are from this country.'

In their sleepy eyes, what do these children comprehend about a country? This country or some other country?' How many countries are there? Which children will feel happy to listen to a rotten word again and again!

Everyone at home ignores his words- let him blabber about the country. When he is tired, he will automatically stop babbling. Once he goes to sleep, he starts snoring. The noise will be all across the house. His grandchildren mock him and say- 'Grandfather sleeps, but from his snore, one can hear Bye! *Bangladesh*, Hi! India.' There was no accountability at home for him. People in the house ignore the children's gossiping.

He gets up from his bed in the afternoons, crosses

the door, and reaches the bank of the river *Gobari*. His eyes get dazed as he rises from a window-less, cave-almost dark, thatched roof house into the setting sunlight of day end; he squeezes his eyes to get some tear (fluid) to see the accurate picture. Then he screams within- 'In the area where my net is spread, my son is standing in that knee-deep slime and is strengthening the net by plugging the poles. On the other side, *Ranjan Jhali* is repairing the broken boat. Eight to ten children from *the Jalipada* colony are playing in that slime. The tidewater is entering into his area slowly through the net. My son is bringing down the net, which was kept on the pole. He goes up and down in that stormy water to set the net properly so the *Vekti or Pabda* fish and crabs can't disappear. After the high tide, the water will recede from the fishing nets into the river. After that, the fish will be scrambling in the dry land. My father had taught me how to earn a living at *Jambu* by fishing on dry land. Now my son is doing the same work.'

- In that country, we had a small grocery shop. I had many times weighed the things and done the billing. In that country, we were businessmen; in this country, we are fishermen. It's surprising. We changed our profession from business people to fishermen to survive in this country. The hand that weighed the things and cleaned the grocery is now working in the slime, repairing the net, and selling fish. My father told me this much before his death- 'Son, our country has changed; our business has changed, so you should change.'

It was almost twilight. It wasn't yet time for all the stars to shine in the sky. One by one, the stars were blooming like flowers in the sky. Looking at the stars, he asks- 'Oh, stars in the sky, do you belong to India or *Bangladesh*? You are above which country? Is it so that stars also have their countries, and compared to them, countries like India and *Bangladesh* are like tiny dust particles? The stars are up above the sky. They sparkle over every nation. He feels as if the stars are his silent audience. He again starts babbling.

-My grandfather secretly participated in the Language Movement in *East Bengal;* that's why the Bihari Muslims had an eye on our house. Sometimes, there was stone pelting; sometimes, my grandfather would be underground. Before the war began, my father brought us to this country. After the war, Indira Gandhi brought a few more people and kept them in *Koraput.* They could not manage there. A group of them shifted from *Koraput* to *Jambu* and stayed with us. We were staying here before Indira Gandhi's *Bangladesh* settlement program. Some of us still need the ration card. It's not only me but almost three hundred people in *Baulakani panchayat* who still need proof certificates of their country.

- My son does petty politics to get a ration card. Let him do that work. My son is also doing good business here. He doesn't belong to any party. When Congress was the ruling party, he belonged to Congress and is now in BJD. He is a follower, depending on which party is in power. He is very clever. He thinks that with the help of the politicians, Revenue Inspector, and *Tehsildar,* he will arrange a ration card. Will we ever get rid of that discredit? I have left the country. The tattoo mark of a dead nation is on my back. The effect will not vanish until I am finished. After my death, no one will call my son a refugee's son is a refugee. My son is born at *Jambu.* He does fishing and petty politics here. After I die as a refugee, he will become a respectable person from a refugee tag.

- 'It's enough about the country. It's already dark, and there is no one around. You are sitting here alone and babbling. Let's go home.' His son said.

He paused at once from the conversation on a country. He was thinking about his son, and he was there. The son took out his mobile to show the light to return home.

After dinner, he would change sides on the bed. His tongue inside the mouth will be desperate and impatient to blabber about the country. He gets a good sleep after he speaks to himself. If he starts talking to his grandchildren, his wife sleeping on the veranda on the other side of the door shouts and says- 'Enough about that useless country talks. Sleep quietly and let the children sleep.'

There is no relief in the dream. Many times, the country enters into his plans. Sometimes, he gets nightmares about his death and gets up midway from his sleep. Open-eyed, he recollects about the half-completed dreams- he sees himself dead in the dream, and none of the two nations is giving permission for his cremation.

Which country will permit his cremation? – He goes to sleep again to complete that half-left-out dream. He gets up before the sunrise every day. Other members of the house would still be sleeping at that moment. He leaves the house towards his fishing net spread out area. At that time, the bank of the river was a little dark and foggy, where one could see someone in the front. He stands near the net spread and thinks at least he has a net –spread in this country. This amount of pride brings some happiness to him. He counts the value of the fish caught in the trap lying on the dryland. Some days, it is possible to console, and others, he fails to do so.

Others occupy much larger fishing net spreads close to his fishing net spread. His father had given it to him, though it was small. But many people need their own net feeds. They work with others. They would call each other to reach their net spreads. Only his son had not arrived. All fathers think alike- that the son is lazy. His thoughts are on the same line. He looked at the fish and crabs trapped in the net, jumping to escape into the river by dragging themselves in the slime water. He gets ready to get into the slime and jumps like a frog so that he will not let the fish and crabs go back into the water. He runs behind a big *Bhekti* fish trapped in the net.

The *Bhekti* fish tries to jump out of the net, and he shouts-' Wait, you scoundrel! You are trying to escape towards the *Gobari* river.' He tries to speak with the fish, enters the knee-deep slime, and grabs it but cannot come out of the mire. In between this ability to emerge from the more, the thoughts about the country spread like clouds within him.

-Yes, I have weighed with the machine in that country, and in this country, the *Bhekti* fish is in my hand. If my father had grown his beard and moustache and dressed up like a Muslim in *Bangladesh*, I would have grown old in my own country. That was the practice during my grandfather and father's time in *East Bengal*. They were forcibly thrusting the religion on others. *Bangladesh* has many big rivers like *Padma, Meghana, Dhleswari, Budhaganga,* and *Madhumati*. They changed the name of the river to -River *Adial Khan*. Let it be, but one among those Muslims was *Sheikh Mujibur Rahman*. The farmers' crops of *East Bengal* would go to Pakistan, and in turn, they got the inedible into the East Bengal. *Mujibur Rahman* was against this. He said – 'Our golden Bengal.' *Sheikh Mujibur Rahman's* powerful speech was broadcast on the radio, and the movement began in 1970. *Mujibur Rahman* became a martyr for the country. *Sheikh Mujibur Rahman* is like *Mahatma Gandhi* of this country. Bengal is a land of sacrifices. From *Khulna, Bidhan Rai, Jyoti Basu, Surya Sen, Maichel Madhusudan, Anukul Chandra, Meghnad Saha,* and *Tapan Sikdar* were the country's jewels. I was born in that country- where gold is harvested.

-One more thing- the people of this country gave us shelter, so we stayed in *Jambu*. If they would have chased us away like in *Bangladesh*, where would we have gone? I was born on the banks of river *Kabataki*, and I will die on the banks of river *Gobari*. I will have only one regret- Not only the people of *Jambu* but also people who live far away in the cities don't have a good notion about us. There is a lot of criticism and bad-mouthing against us. They think that we have acquired the forest land near river *Gobari*. Many believe that the people living in *Jambu* are *Bangladeshi* Muslims. A few newspapers also print that we are involved in spying for *Bangladesh*. We are smuggling medicinal plants from here illegally, hunting deer. We are engaged in illegal activities like human trafficking and printing fake currency. We are blamed for all the evil deeds in this country- All from *Bangladesh* are rogues!

-' Who is saying that all the *Bangladeshi*s are rogues? Who?

Early in the morning, when a few *Bangladeshi*s overheard about this, they would leave their work on other netspread and come to fight. Then they would see him knee-deep in the slime with a *Bhekti* fish in his hand and unable to go off the dirt. Only he talks about the country. On his way from the house to the fishing net spread, his idle son could find many people gathered around his net space. He came running and saw that his father could not escape the slime. He was holding a *Bhekti* fish and talking about the country.

His son immediately entered the dirt, pulled him up, and made him sit in the dry land.

-' The way he always talks about India and *Bangladesh*, one day he will be the reason for a fight between the *Maedeinpur Bengalis* and *Bangladeshis*.'

-' Take him to the hospital in *Cuttack*.'

The son sees his neighbours advising him about his father. His son could see his father sitting with his legs spread, covered with slime. The son looked at him and thought- 'Is he harming anyone? He is speaking to himself. How can he be called insane? He works with the fence like a craftsman and tells the story to his grandchildren about the countries. He is engaged in talking to himself on the banks of river Gobari or at home. He is always happy and busy with his work. Why will he be insane? He caught a *Bhekti* fish to increase his family's income. How can he be mad?'

One of them advised-' Take him to the doctor and give him proper treatment.'

- 'Go and do your work. Which doctor and medicine can help in removing the country from his head? Let him be there. Let him be as he is.'

∞∞∞∞∞∞∞∞∞∞∞

Glossary

- **Lungi-** A garment wrapped around the waist and extending to the ankles

- **Baul Sangeet-** Bauls are a group of mystic minstrels or bards of mixed elements of Sufism and Sahaja from the Bengal region.

- **Sonar Bangla-** Golden Bengal

- **Dismil-** Land measurement unit

- **Verandah-** A roofed platform along the outside of a house

- **Guntha-** Land measurement unit

- **Bhekti:** A freshwater fish (Asian Seabass Fish)

Black Eagle Books

www.blackeaglebooks.org
info@blackeaglebooks.org

Black Eagle Books, an independent publisher, was founded as a nonprofit organization in April, 2019. It is our mission to connect and engage the Indian diaspora and the world at large with the best of works of world literature published on a collaborative platform, with special emphasis on foregrounding Contemporary Classics and New Writing.

www.ingramcontent.com/pod-product-compliance
Lightning Source LLC
Chambersburg PA
CBHW020150120726
47903CB00007B/2483